CRUNK

By

BAD BOYZ

Tariq • Rudd • Jones

Black Pearl Books Publishing

WWW.BLACKPEARLBOOKS.COM

CRUNK

By Bad Boyz (Tariq – Rudd – Jones)

Published By:

BLACK PEARL BOOKS INC.

3653-F FLAKES MILL ROAD – PMB 306
ATLANTA, GA 30034
404-735-3553

All Black Pearl Books titles, imprints and distributed lines are available at special quantity discounts for bulk purchases for sales promotion, premiums, fund raising, educational or institutional use.

Special book excerpts or customized printings can also be created to fit specific needs. For details, write to Black Pearl Books: Attention Senior Publisher, 3653-F Flakes Mill Road, PMB-306, Atlanta, Georgia 30034 or visit website: www.BlackPearlBooks.com

FOR DISTRIBUTOR INFO & BULK ORDERING

Contact: Black Pearl Books, Inc.
              3653-F Flakes Mill Road
              PMB 306
              Atlanta, Georgia 30034
              404-735-3553

Discount Book-Club Orders via website:

www.BlackPearlBooks.com

ISBN: 0-9728005-3-0

Publication Date: January 2005

Cover Credits

Design: CANDACEK. (WWW.CCWEBDEV.COM)

CRUNK

By

Tariq • Rudd • Jones

Black Pearl Books Publishing

www.BlackPearlBooks.com

ACKNOWLEDGEMENTS - Tariq

I give thanks to Allah that this project evolved into a finished product. All praise is due to Him and I openly confess that I am indeed grateful for the gift of imagination and the ability to put the images in my head onto paper.

I am deeply indebted to my family, The Brown Tribe. I love them all. My parents: Evans and Maggaline, my sisters: Charlotte, Lorraine, Jacqueline, Valerie, Carolyn, Gwendolyn, Angela, Paula. My brothers: Buddy Cool, Bro. Dave (Qayyam). My tribe within the tribe. My daughters: LaTonya, Adrienne, Shameka, Aisha, Latifa. My son, Hakim. Their children: Floyd Jr., Isiah, Destiny. My nieces: LaTasha, Nikki, Tara, Tamara, Keisha, Megan, Dequasha. My nephews: Charles "Chuck" Anthony, Travis, Tee, Dewan, Ricky, Gene, DJ, Haywood, Xavier, Malik.

I also salute and extend my love to the other branches of the family: The Millers, The Blackmons, The Morris'.

I must thank Mrs. Joan Boudreax, the best English teacher in the world. She taught me all I know and was the first one to believe in me. Without her, I would have quit. Thanks, Mrs. B. for not giving up on me.

Big respect to all my comrades-in-chains. Forrest "PeeWee" Malker, Emerson "Moor" Ledwell-Bey, Antwain Wells, Leroy "Country" Alexander, Zulu Moore, Louis Medley, Big E. Jones, Claude Miler, Whop, Ras Cecil, C. "Divine" Singleton, Bomani, Jondi "J" Harrell, Big Richard Neely, Tyree, Bro. Scientific, Big O & the NC Crew, Beech, Tick, Wayne (Al), Dontay, Dee, Rusty Bolder, Terry Blackmon, Jeff "Barnyard" Brown, Ears, Zeke, Fabian McDearis, Vic, Nicky, Allan Poulnott, Norman Dean, Nate, Atl, Furr, Taco, PJ Laney, Big Reg, Flint-El, Billy D., CoCo, Big Swole, Mike Hamms, Taha, and the rest of the B-1 cellblock. Peace 2 all. Also Boston, Lightfoot and Allen Chapman. A Special Shout Out 2 my cellie, Carl "Shorty" Glover who has been like a brother 2 me since we first met at arion 25 years ago. Oh yeah. I can't forget Shahid and the Wake-up orderly crew!

It is vital that I salute my partners-in-prose, Gregory "Bo" Jones and Gregory Rudd, who are true literary geniuses. May Allah reward these brothas and their loved ones. I will stand with them 4ever.

Free Dr. Mutulu Shakur and all Political Prisoners.

Thanks to Vibe Magazine for giving due props to "Street Lit".

Orleander Love, Martin Russell, Haywood Peele, Joseph "TreeTop" Hamm, Marty Rorie. Inshallah, I will holla soon!

Lastly, Ups to Felicia Hurst and Black Pearl Books for realizing the potential of this work and moving it into print quickly. ALLAH-U-AKBAR!

ACKNOWLEDGEMENTS - Rudd

All praise first due to Allah for life, guidance and direction.

I give much love to my mother (Shirley Rudd-Johnson). I wish you were here to see this. To my children (Zaakirah, Ahmads, Kaliyah and Takeemah), dad loves you and cannot wait to get home to you.

To Ali, Bo, Dr. Shakur, my partners in words and life, thanks for holding me down.

To Khalil (Phila.), Saheed (BX, NY), Sabree, thanks for the wise words. Nafi and Fateem, love y'all for always being there. Bro. Shabazz, don't worry I got you. Latif aka Notty and Abdul aka Goonbey, many years, many tears, love is love. Kazm aka North Philly, Abdul, D.C., Storm.

My homies-Black the Bronx is safe now, love you, son. Divine the king of New York. Gee, B.K. to the fullest. Sony and Panama-N.Y.C. and that boy Bezo, Mr. Young, C.T., Big Zee and that boy J.B., Big B, MMorse Man, P.A., The Bowling Team, Bald Head, Big Q., Philly J., Doc, Oregon, Nelly, S.C., Tx Black, Boo, NC, Bro Marvin, Morris Green-Fla., Drama and Gee Blood IN, Blood Out., Pork Chop, my brother from the other mother. Bro. Tony, now let us Pray, Pop. Gee-Motor City, Dean, a real good guy. C.L. – P.A., Rap on, Rap on. Abraham McDowell and Tirrell, NW-D.C., Big David, Ears, BeBe, Big E., Eric, Zeek, Yam Yam.

Yo, if I didn't get you, I didn't mean to miss you. Love is Love!

Still In Da Game But Changed The Name

ACKNOWLEDGEMENTS - Jones

Through my faith and belief, I first must give Thanks to "The Almighty Creator" and my ancestors who are always with me in spirit.

It is evident as described in the pages of another book, how grateful I am to have Linda (My Wife) in my life. You have always stood in my corner. Also my deepest gratitude goes to my kids (Kent, Ungenits and Arleshia) for giving me so much joy.

I expecially thank my mother Ozella and my aunts Ann & Gloria for their mental support.

Also, thanks is given to other members of my family for their love (Tytiana, Shawnquavius, Ungenits, Reginald, Sam Mozell, Dee Dee, Little Ratt, Mable, Shirley, Bernice, Gaynell, June Bug, Pinkin, James, Willie, Catfish, Gary, Joyce, Johnny, Gabrielle, Gary Jr., Gavin, Kim, Gayla, Jerald, Tan Tan, Quincy, Tanisha, Terrel, La Nikka, Sharmaine, Felicia, Jarnard, Shanta, Chanell, Marcus, Tieyonner) and also my late (Grandmother-Mrs. Pricella Boswell and my Mother-In-Law – Mrs. Geraldine Beech) who I pray is resting in peace. You are forever remembered.

Thanks to all at Black Pearl Books and most especially to Ms. Felicia Hurst for the support and belief in "CRUNK". Thank you again for this opportunity.

Additionally, I wish to shout out tomy USP-Brothers (Calvin Thomas, Tracey E. Squaire, Alan Poulnott, emerson Ledwell-Bey, Ahmad Shabazz Muhammed, Theodous Williams, Othis Hasty, Frank Sharpe, Terry C. Jenkins, Quenton "Joe" Thompson, Lehmon Hunt, Lake Charles, Terry English, Dr. Mutulu Shakur, Ricardo Finkley, Cyril Melton, Keith "Beech" Martin, Ricco Crump, Edward "Billy Dee" Williams, Leroy "Country" Alexander, Clarence Snoop"Aaron, Lucious "Luke" Boswell-Madison/GA, Mac Holstick, Lawrence Martin, Lucky, Robert Boyd, Monstsho E. Vernon, Reginald Paris, Lil Furr, John "Duke" Queen, Gilyard, Joe Joe, Antonio Sadler, andre Lark, Tyrone Carter, Louis Medley, Maurice Martin-233, Ernest Carter, Alvoy Wright-II and Jay. Please forgive me for those I missed. And also Antwain Wells and Big M. Brown.

To Coop Jr., from WRFG 89.3 FM in Atlanta, I have mad respect for you. Thanks for giving us our first book interview.

A special thanks is sent to Mr. Troy Johnson, Founder of AALBC.com, (African-American Literary Book Club). Thank you again for the work you did in setting up our web page.

And finally but not least of all, I owe a grateful thanks to my two co-authors Gibran Tariz and Gregory Rudd. I enjoyed toh insights and wisdom we shared in making this possible, may your future novels be fruitful.   --To All Again Thanks!

Chapter 1

A fine misty rain fell gently upon the 12th District, that long stretch of Interstate-85 that snaked through North Carolina between Raleigh and Charlotte, squeezing all the other cities in the middle of them like a metropolitan sandwich topped with poverty and violence.

Raleigh and Charlotte were the two superpowers in the Tar Heel State, a pair of concrete and steel jungles that still maintained their southern plantation mentality, and who were still quick on the draw when it came to filling up the 100 prisons that dotted the country landscape.

However, none of this mattered to the occupants of the black Escalade with New York tags. They weren't into the history of the State. Could've cared less about the great basketball tradition of Duke and Carolina. As a matter of fact, the occupants of the Escalade were true ride and die niggas and they were on a mission. More precisely, their plan was to man-handle the whole South and put it on lock, to make the southern niggas bow down.

"Where we at now?", Bone asked. "Seem like we been riding long enough to be in Jerusalem by now. You sho' we ain't lost 'cause if we is, you gotta pull this bitch over 'bout dark. This the Dirty South and I hear they don't play that shit down here with niggas out after the sun done gone down"

Robot laughed, "Man, you need to chill with that Gone With The Wind shit. The Bottom ain't like that no mo'. Niggas down here be doing the same thing we be doing up top. They just be doing it slower"

"And with a goddamn country-assed drawl", Kool G. laughed. "Niggas' accent be so corny, it's almost like them Bamas are from a different country"

"If it's like that", Red Devil, the driver, commented, "then we can't help but come-up"

"But what if we don't know where the fuck we at?"

Red Devil shook his head. "See what happens when you take a nigga out of Harlem for the first time. Motherfucka don't see none of the landmarks and he 'bout to go crazy"

"What the fuck you expect? I ain't seen shit but tall ass trees for the last two hours. Where are the goddamn big buildings at?"

"Fool, we on the Interstate, not cruising up 125th Street"

"Still-------"

"Read that big, goddamned, green-ass sign, Bone", Red Devil sighed. "What the fuck it say, 90 miles to Charlotte?"

"Thank you Jah, and pass that blunt"

Without looking, Kendra picked up the phone.

"Put KoKo on"

Kendra tossed the cordless to the young, handsome man sitting on the sofa.

"Yo, KoKo here"

"Danger, cuz"

"What up, Shine. Run it past me"

"This just came through a pair of lips who heard it from the horse's mouth"

"I feel you cuz, so spit it"

"Niggas from Harlem en route, bringing drama"

KoKo bolted upright. "What niggas?"

"Don't get me to lying 'cause I can't call it. All I know is that the peeps ain't from Crooklyn, but if I had to take a guess, I wouldn't. It could be any one of these niggas up in Harlem who be throwing up they set, but man, what you acting surprised about? Harlem done got so sissified it's almost like Mayberry. Motherfuckingcrackers everywhere, sitting out on the stoop like they white asses were born in the hood. Anyway, niggas done picked up the habit of exporting the drama south"

"Well, it's a goddamn bad habit"

"That's what your mouth say, cuz, but everybody think y'all niggas down there soft as the cotton the slaves used to pick. And Charlotte, man, it ain't even on the radar. For real, cuz, ain't nobody repping the hood down there. I mean that's where Jodeci from, but them niggas busted up, so who else y'all got to holla for y'all? No-fucking-body"

"Nigga, life ain't no goddamn talent show. What, 'cause a hood ain't got some fool ass niggas in no music videos with a rack of silly bitches shaking they salt shakers, that don't mean shit. Niggas roll up down heah, thinking this some American Idol shit, I guarantee they gonna get flat-blasted"

"Don't talk me to death", Shine laughed, " 'cause I ain't got nuthin' but love for you"

3

"My bad, cuz, I'm just venting. Who told you that shit anyway?"

"Jalisa, my baby mama. Her other baby daddy swing wit' the crew who on the road coming your way. She heard the nigga on the horn"

"And she sho' they said Charlotte?"

"That's why she brought the bone to me. She remembered last summer when me and her came down and spent the weekend with you. Remember how you spoiled the shit out of her and our lil' shorty, and she told you that she was going to pay you back one day for your generosity. Well, she just did. Niggas on the way, cuz"

KoKo rubbed his temples. "All I can say is that this them niggas last ride"

"Handle your biz'ness then. I'm out"

"Later"

KoKo checked his watch while he prayed that Coot would hurry up and answer his phone.

"Yo"

" 'Bout time. You real busy?"

Coot grunted. "As long as all the dollar bills in Raleigh ain't in my pockets, then hell the fuck yeah, I'm real busy. Why, you wanna give me some of that paper from out of Charlotte?"

"Look, Coot, I got some New York niggas trying to ride ghost on me. Fools think NC soft as cotton"

"Word?"

"For sho'. I just found out. And you know that if they take Charlotte, they gonna kick the hinges off of Raleigh's ass next. So I say we posse up"

"Bet that. Niggas better push on to Atlanta"

"Motherfuckas kinda scared of the ATL. Them Dirty South boys down there done got crunk"

"Then what the fuck we waiting on? Let's get crunk the fuck up and hit them bitches up wit' some good ol' southern hospitality. You feel that?"

"No doubt, but right now what I need you to do is to tack a tail on them niggas. They on zoom coming down 85"

"Where at?"

"That I don't know, but hit Rip and Moto 'cause the motherfuckas might be done shot past Raleigh. If so, Rip and Moto can pick they asses up. I'll ding-a-ling Trueblood in Salisbury and have him post some niggas up. Trueblood ain't but 'bout 45 miles from me and I don't believe they done got that close that quick"

"What they pushing?"

"Black Escalade. NY-tags"

"I'm about it"

"Coot?"

"Yeah?"

"Just tail 'em. Don't fuck with 'em and don't spook 'em. I'll keep my phone line open so we can have clear communication. I want to know what those bitches doing every stop of the way"

"Then what?"

"When they get heah, I'm gonna welcome they ass to the Queen City real proper"

"I heard that", Coot laughed. "Boy, this might set off another Civil War, only this time it'll be between thugs"

"Only this time, the North won't win"

Coot laughed again. "Motherfucking history teacher said that the South was gonna rise again"

"But this probably ain't what he was talking 'bout"

"How the fuck you know. Cracker might've been fucking Miss Cleo or something and seen this shit coming. Later"

KoKo spent the next half of the afternoon on the phone, listening to Rip and Moto give him the 4-1-1 on the New York visitors who were still on the bounce zooming down 85 right into the eye of the storm.

KoKo liked the way he saw the episode playing out. He would take the fight out of these niggas by taking the fight to them and in the process send a chilling message back up North that the Low-down brothas from the Down-Low were not to be tampered with.

Irregardless of the consequences, KoKo felt that he had to sacrifice these niggas for the sake of all the ballers in the Bottoms, but he knew that the killings couldn't be mere grandstanding because niggas could stomach death better than anybody else on the planet, so he had to commit a murder that would say that it wasn't a good idea to mess with crunk niggas from the low-end of the country.

"Motherfuckas just don't know they taking they last ride", Moto laughed. "Fools riding right into the boneyard and don't even know it"

"They'll know soon enough"

"Just don't let 'em shake you or nuthin' and I promise to make the whole South proud when they touch down"

"Throw up your set then, nigg. Rep Charlotte. Take them niggas' cookies"

Red Devil's mind was on his next stop, Charlotte. He figured he could conquer everything on his agenda minus a whole lot of mayhem. Southern niggas were wack, modern day dirt farmers, long-time squares, but it would still be a great victory for Harlem, another link in the chain to extend the reach of New York across the nation.

"These punks probably won't even put up a fight. They in awe of playas from up top, so they'll surrender like a virgin with a couple of shots of Hennessey in her"

Red Devil turned on the radio, "Listen to that shit"

"That's crunk", Bone responded.

"What?!"

"Crunk, Southern funk and rap"

"Whatever it is, it ain't got no flava" Red Devil screwed up his nose in disgust. "Where that jive start at?"

"Atlanta-------"

"No fucking wonder", Red Devil complained. "The South ain't shit. Niggas down here slow as Christmas. Do you know how much paper it is in the South and yet you got them Uncle Tom busters working at McDonald's"

Robot turned pensive. "On the up and up, once we take over that spot, I'm thinking that it would be a good gift to give to our women. You know, move 'em down here"

"You have got to be bullshitting?"

"Why not, a kid needs space to grow up. Grass down here all pretty and green. You know what I see the South as--a great big ol' park. I can't speak for the rest of y'all but this is where I want my shorties to grow up"

7

"Not me", Kool G. cracked. "Bring my kids down here and then be needing an interpreter when they start talking just so you can understand that country-assed drawl"

The majority of the niggas KoKo had called up were from off the Westside, down by Beatties Ford Road, past Johnson C. Smith University, but the small crew from out of North Carolina were the heart of the thug world because they were the most deadly. This morning KoKo needed the North Charlotte posse just to watch his back. He would use his Westside posse as the actual attack force because he had known most of these niggas since he was a pee-wee and he knew they all were both loyal and ferocious. They were all killers.

But KoKo himself was no stranger to killing although he preferred to use it only as a military strategy and never as a tool for personal vendettas. In fact, KoKo considered being emotional a weakness because when a thug took shit personal, it became hard for him to distinguish between his appetites and his ambitions. Therefore, no emotions excited him, no earthly beauty or pleasure distracted him, and no man, so far, had frightened him.

Kenny, "KoKo" Combs was tall, thin and dark. He played with ideas the way most men flirted with bitches, and he dreamed of being the greatest thug the South had ever produced. He almost got a nut just thinking about building an empire that stretched throughout the whole bottom half of the Mason-Dixon Line. He had visions of his Storm Troopers establishing turf in Charlotte and then marching on to new territories in Virginia and South Carolina. Then from there he would extend his reach as well as his wealth and power all over the South.

KoKo had always carried his weight on the Westside mainly through his fiery magnetism, but now with the coming of the empty-heads from up North this just might be the perfect time to change the course of thug history.

"There is also the possibility that we might have to check them ATL niggas to", Bandit confided to KoKo. "They believe that they the cream of the crop down in the Dirty South, that they better than all the rest of us. You see how them busters act when we show up down there. Even the bitches be acting like our dicks crooked or something"

Though KoKo remained silent, he knew there was some truth to what his right-hand man had whispered in his ear. "One thang at a time, partner", he finally replied. "One thang at a time"

Back on the highway, the Escalade hit the city limits of Charlotte about late-afternoon. Robot nudges Bone, who had been in a deep doze for the last 30 miles.

"Wake up, Sleeping Beauty", he teased, "we done touched down in Bamaville. What you gotta say about that?"

"Pull the fuck over so I can get something to eat. That's what"

And so it was shortly after the black Escalade with the NY tags had pulled into Wendy's on Freedom Drive that KoKo got the phone call he had been waiting for.

"The buzzards have landed", he said, calling his troops together. "No surrender", he commanded. "No retreat and no one gets out alive"

Thus inspired, the Westside Connection, followed closely by the crew from North Carolina hit the road.

Bone looked up with his mouth full. "Hey, look at them country-assed motherfuckas hanging around our ride"

"Chill out, Bone. Damn, as long as they ain't trying to steal it, we cool. Niggas probably ain't never seen no whip like that down here. This NASCAR country, you dig, so motherfuckas probably bugging the fuck out 'cause our shit so out of control"

Bone took another bite of his cheeseburger, then gazed back out of the squeaky clean plate glass window. "Oh, hell the fuck, naw. That bama know his country ass wrong, leaning up against our whip like he ain't got good sense" Bone jumped up. "I ain't having it. Let's go confront these farmboys"

Bandit, who was squatting down, glanced up at the four New Yorkers with awe in his eyes. "Man, what kinda rims is these?"

"Too much for your country ass to think about paying for them. Now, get the fuck up and get in the wind", Bone cracked. "Ain't y'all got some cotton to pick" He cocked his head to the side and cupped his hand to his ear as though listening. "I think I hear Mr. Bo-Bo, the Massa, calling your black ass. You hear him?"

In a flash, Bandit was up, having snatched his 9mm out. "That's funny, all I hear is the clack of these pieces me and my boys got. That's what I hear"

Bandit nodded and the New Yorkers were quickly shoved into four different cars and driven off into the sunset.

Inside the lead car, Heart-beat slapped Bone. "Bitch-assed nigga, think about how good your life used to be 'cause the motherfucka just about to come to a close. You and your peeps about to get crunked!"

Chapter 2

Moses London had been an undertaker for several decades. He had served as the funeral director for some of New York's finest, from the high-steppers up on Striver's Row and Sugar Hill to the low-lifes down in the bowels of Harlem, but during all the time he had never believed it would be possible for him to see bodies so mutilated that it would make him vomit, until now.

The bodies of the four men looked like they had been a medical experiment gone bad. The youngest had his eyes plucked out of his head, one had his ears cut off. Another had experienced the agony of having his nose sliced from his face while the last one had suffered through having his throat ripped open. But that was the pretty part. The executioners had dubbed it the E.E.N.T. (Ear, Eyes, Nose, and Throat) process.

In case anyone in Harlem struggled with the ugly lessons offered by the E.E.N.T., there was the eye-grabbing reminder left by the word CRUNK that had been viciously carved across each of the for men's chest. The letters were two inches deep and more than three inches wide, each alphabet increasing the power and ugliness of the one coming next.

Moses realized and accepted that whoever had committed this atrocity had considered it a great honor to perform the duty and was, more than likely, held in high esteem by whoever it was that had ordered the brutal mutilations. Unfortunately, there was not much he could do to reconstruct most of the disorder and damage done to the badly mangled bodies, but at least he could reattach the facial parts.

"Only a master of disaster would have ordered something like this", Moses quietly explained to Rah-Rah Tillman, the stoic man paying for the funerals. "Someone 100% evil"

Rah-Rah was not interested in the man's philosophy and he wanted to keep the talk to a bare minimum so he rudely cut the mortician off.

"The letter? That's what I'm here for" Rah-Rah didn't want to waste any time. He wanted to read the note and to decipher the danger he faced because as leader of the crew from New York, he needed to see quickly what he had gotten himself into.

"You do have it handy, don't you?"

"Yes", Moses said politely, "I have it and that is why I called you. I figured it could be of much importance to you"

"The sooner you give it to me, the sooner I can see about that," Rah-Rah snapped gruffly. "Now, please get it"

"Wait right here"

When Moses returned a few moments later, he thrust a folded up slip of paper at Rah-Rah.

"It was shoved in one of your friend's mouth"

Unfolding the letter, Rah-Rah knew it would give him a lot to consider and reconsider, but he felt that the first thing he had to do would be to make an example out of someone. He wanted to hang the motherfucka responsible for the slaughter of his men.

Seeing Rah-Rah's hands tremble, Moses gripped the young man's hands tightly between his own.

"This letter contains unspeakable evil, Rah-Rah. Once you open it and peek at whatever is written within, you will never be the same"

"Then so be it," Rah-Rah growled.

But Moses wanted a clear conscience. "I had known your father all his life and one night right here in this exact same room, I saw him with fire and blood in his eyes. Just like you. I tried to save him from something that was bigger than him, but my begging only made resolve stronger. Now, I beg you to leave this thing alone whatever it is. It will eat you alive"

Rah-Rah roughly snatched his hands away. "I am not my father"

Moses nodded his assent. "I know. You are even a bigger fool"

"Rah-Rah opened the letter. It read"

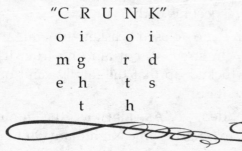

```
"C  R  U  N  K"
 o  i     o  i
 m  g     r  d
 e  h     t  s
    t     h
```

Immediately after the funeral Rah-Rah used the chapel to hold his meeting with the thugs he had invited up from Jersey, Philly, and DC. It was his hope to unite all the niggas up top because he would need them to help carve out a toehold in Virginia which would allow him to muscle his way back into

15

Carolina or either invade Tennessee to the west. He had heard that Memphis was sweet.

After being up all night Rah-Rah was happy about his chances of gaining these niggas support and even though he was cool with the fact that their primary duty was to their home turf, he was sure that if he showed how he could make them all richer by dividing the South up among themselves, he was convinced he would easily win them over.

The two men he was closest to, Mustapha out of Jersey, and Dream from Philly, offered him mad condolences and were prepared to get down to business. Whop, from DC, the most high-spirited of the three visitors was more ready to party and celebrate.

To lighten the mood, Rah-Rah fired up a blunt and spoke slowly. "Y'all saw it with your own eyes. Niggas butchered up like they were swine. The dead brothas were all good soldiers, but they were outmanned and outgunned, but you still don't fuck up a man's body like that. We all know that if you capture a hope-to-die thug in battle and you gotta do him, you put a single bullet in his head. That's on F.P., out of respect but you see what them square-assed country niggas did. They out of law. It's one thing to kill a thug, but something else to disrespect his body"

"But it wasn't no closed casket funeral," Dream reminded Rah-Rah. "In street war it ain't no true diss until they do the body so fucked up that the family can't open the casket. Ain't that how it go?"

Mustapha nodded. "As long as the family not disrespected by some extra gruesome Nightmare On Elm Street type shit, all is fair. Every thug deserves a righteous burial so as long as the family and the crew can look the deceased in the face, then the killer done gave up props"

"Plus the wrong on you, my man", Dream remarked calmly, "if your peeps went down there to spread death. You can't invade new turf if you ain't 100% strapped. Your peeps came up short 'cause they slept on them southern boys. ", Dream shrugged. "I pride myself on stepping up to the plate when the beef concerns Philly, but if you gonna ask for muscle ..."

Rah-Rah looked shocked.

"Damn, Dream, I thought I could count on you for your support"

Dream started to scream on Rah-Rah, but since he felt the nigga's pain, he remained composed.

"Look, let me tell you what's happening in the Big Illy"

"Dream, look man, I ain't coming at none of y'all with my hat in my hands. I wanna share with you the greatest prize in the country, the South. So this ain't begging, this is a special request to help ourselves to untold riches and unheard of thug glory. I'm a true believer that if we posse up that we can conquer The Bottom"

Rah-Rah spoke with great enthusiasm because he knew that his three visitors were all impressed by the great wealth of the South, not to mention the phat, cornbread fed bitches down there who sported donkey asses.

Rah-Rah painted an elaborate portrait of a paradise on earth, millions and millions of dollars, magnificently tricked-out, whips, and homes with thousands and thousands of square feet so elegant they would make Donald Trump jealous.

"This is it dawgs, the big picture. Sure, we getting paper and we all got a life up here in the North, but the South represents the thug after life, how a motherfucka supposed to live after a life in the trenches. Man, the South is a pilgrimage that we gotta make and it's ours for the taking", Rah-Rah smiled with affection at his guests.

"We can carve up the Dirty Down like it's a Thanksgiving Turkey"

Rah-Rah turned to Whop. "You been quiet so far, brer. What's the good word?"

Whop stood, stretching his imposing physique to it's maximum height. He took a slight breath.

"You talk a good game, but tell me this. If we was to posse up the whole up top who we gonna be paying our loyalty to as the Top Dawg of the family? New York?"

Rah-Rah sputtered, not expecting that question. "Wh-when the time comes to choose a Top Dawg, then the thug best suited to preside over our pilgrimage should get the spot" Rah-Rah smiled faintly. "Is this your way of letting us know that DC campaigning for the presidency?"

"Naw, dawg, it ain't like that," Whop scowled, 'cause DC don't need shit from nobody"

"Then what your beef is?"

"Family. What you don't recognize is that DC can't roll on NC 'cause we cousins"

"How the fuck you figure that? You North, they South. No offense Whop", Rah-Rah laughed, "but I think you got your geography twisted. The District is above the Mason-Dixon Line"

"No offense taken brotha, but this the thing. Damn near every nigga in DC got family in North Carolina. The truth is that most of the people in DC come out of NC. Two out of three DC niggas will tell you quick that they Mama or they grandmama was born in Carolina, so you see we blood with them niggas down there. They may be country, but they cuz, you dig?"

"So, what you saying?"

"What, did I stutter or something? What part of that you didn't understand Rah-Rah? DC ain't getting down with your ass and I don't think I can make it no plainer than that"

"Cool, dawn, I can respect that," Rah-Rah then waved his hands in dismissal. "You can roll out, man. Peace Out"

Whop stepped towards Rah-Rah. "Bitch nigga. You got life fucked up if you think you can dismiss me like I'm some bitch"

Dram blocked Whop's path and leaning close, whispered in the brotha from DC's ear. Whop relaxed. And so did Rah-Rah who didn't want an enemy as ruthless as either of the three thugs, so Rah-Rah was careful to issue Whop a big apology.

When the tension was smoothed over, Dream took the floor. The brotha from Philly had an illustrious reputation for always keeping both eyes open and staying two steps ahead of everyone else. When he spoke his voice boomed.

"Failure to show up today in your time of need would have been unthuglike so here I am"

Rah-Rah nodded. "Thanks, Dream, for showing love?"

"But I can't commit no soldiers to this adventure of yours, my comrade"

Rah-Rah frowned. "The South is full of paper and bitches"

"And I don't doubt that and I dig bitches and money just like the next rugged thug, but I got beef on my own doorstep, and that's what makes my own journey so hard. Everybody on the East Coast done heard about what went down with Boo and Tommy and the bloodshed ain't nowhere near finished yet" Dream stared at Rah-Rah. "Got my own cross to bear, you dig?"

Rah-Rah couldn't believe his bad luck. "What about you, Mustapha?"

Behind Dream, Mustapha stood up. He towered over everyone else in the room; big, wide-shoulder and black as the Ace-of-Spades.

"All bullshit aside, Rah, I don't know why you even called me from the get-go. You know how y'all New York niggas look down on Jersey, acting like we ain't got our own

19

thang, like we ain't no real estate, but just the outskirts of the Big Apple. Shit crazy. Y'all treat us like we hoes when we come across to do business, so don't be fronting. You know y'all niggas call us country and it was all good until now when you don' found some more motherfuckas more country than us"

Rah-Rah couldn't believe any of this, but Mustapha continued to rant.

"We right next door to you, but whenever we try to partner up with y'all, what do you niggas do -- give us y'all ass to kiss. And now you got the goddamn nerve to call on us for aid and assistance" Mustapha shook his head vigorously. "I don't think so"

The three men walked out.

Now that Rah-Rah had set his destiny in motion, he knew he must walk the walk even though DC, Philly, and Jersey had left him hanging. He was already committed to combat with those country Bamas, so if his word as a true thug was to remain untarnished, Rah-Rah knew he still had to invade The Bottom.

He was vulnerable without the thug alliance he had hoped for, but he could still destroy the South with his own Troopers if he... Rah-Rah decided to quit fooling himself. He needed support. Granted, his Harlem crew had a cruel streak and most were battle-tested vets, but still, standing alone, the niggas lacked enough fire to carry the war by their lonesome.

Rah-Rah felt like getting pissy drunk, but what fucking purpose would that serve? Whiskey sure as hell wouldn't make his problem disappear. Not hardly, so he just as well quit faking. This was the biggest challenge of his life and here he was on the verge of coming up short. After a shot of gin and juice, he felt obliged to seek the opinion of someone else. He lowered his head when he spoke.

"What would you do if you were in my position, Justice?"

The light-skinned man, with a tiny smirk on his face, replied candidly.

"Ain't but one way to play it, homeboy. To get our foot in the door down there we gonna need an alliance.'

Didn't I just finish telling you what them back-stabbing niggas pulled on me?"

Justice smiled, "Fuck them. Plus that ain't what I'm talking 'bout no how" Justice walked over and placed his hand reassuringly on Rah-Rah's shoulder.

"The ATL is the key. Isolate them motherfuckas and we own the cookie store"

"Nigga, I ain't shamed to say that you done lost me"

"Naw, I ain't," Justice confessed, "you just ain't put all the pieces of the puzzle together yet, but here it is. Just like that nigga Mustapha said that New York niggas think we the cream of the crop up North, well, them thugs from Atlanta feel like they the shit down South and them other southern fried gangstas can't stand it. And that's why all the other niggas in the South don't dig motherfuckas from the ATL, so there it is, our backdoor. We partner up with the ATL. You think they give a fuck about Charlotte or Memphis or any of them other little hick spots in the Bottom? We pull them Georgia dudes in and let 'em know off the top that we ain't got no beef with them and that we'll cut them in on the takedown' man, it'll all be butter between us"

Rah-Rah jumped up, bear hugging his lieutenant.

"Nigga, you brilliant. That's the motherfucking solution to the goddamn problem" Rah-Rah whooped and cheered wildly.

A Bad Boyz Novel
"If this ain't the beginning of the motherfucking end for them second-class country thugs, then I don't know what is"

Chapter 3

"To those less fortunate then we are!"

And with those words, Bandit popped the cork on the bottle of the ultra-expensive champagne, spraying the bubbly all over the breasts and butts of the scantily clad dancers. The girls shrieked with pleasure.

Everyone had fun and games on their minds except KoKo. As a bonafide southern thug he felt he knew a little something about the nature of payback. It was more than just the bitch, men said it was. Payback was a desperate monster that helped thugs keep score of the dead bodies and when it came time for him to greet the greedy, unseeing beast KoKo simply prayed that him and his boys were on the winning side of this unpleasant obligation. But who knew how shit would play out.

They were in one of the exclusive VIP rooms at Champagne's and though the drinks flowed, the bitches were phat, and the music crunk, none of this made KoKo forget that some New York niggas still existed and until he had slaughtered them all------- at least the ones that threatened the South ------- he would not celebrate.

Every time he tried to excuse himself from the partying, one of the fine bitches would dance for him and he would politely watch even though he wasn't turned on. He stayed merely to pacify his crew.

As KoKo observed another dirty dance, he applauded cheerfully when the girl pulled back her G-string, exposing her bald-headed pussy.

First Bandit and then J-Jo stuck their fingers into the girl's vagina, rubbing and caressing her as she gyrated her hips seductively. Then it was Spook Daddy's turn.

Bo-Jack followed as Big Dee gleefully awaited his turn.

When the girl got to KoKo, he smiled and rubbed her phat ass instead. She pouted and moved on. Glad he hadn't offended the sista, KoKo retreated back into his private thoughts. Partying had little or damn near nothing to do with his destiny. What he intended to claim from life was fame and fortune and not hardly the joys that were based on a woman's flesh. A nigga could take your woman, but he could never steal your legacy.

He thought about shit. Today, his enemies in New York had been in mourning, laying their soldiers to rest and tonight, here they were celebrating what they had did to those soldiers. Life was funny because KoKo knew that if he slipped, niggas in the Big Apple would be swapping stories about what they had done to him and his boys. But such was fate.

As he knew he soon would, he said a brainstorm, one that might keep him out of a casket. He guessed that now was as good a time as any to get the train on track.

"Excuse me, party people but I gotta go handle something"

Bandit escorted KoKo to the door of the VIP room. "What up, homey. You gotta get them bitch niggas off your mind and enjoy yourself. Them niggas gonna be our footstool"

"That's the shit I be wanting to hear. I'll holla. I'm gonna call my cuz in Crooklyn"

At first Shine objected to the plan, but he's starting sing a different tune once KoKo beautified the conversation with dollar signs.

"That much?"

"Yeah, cuz, that much"

"That's a whole lot of cake. You holding like that you should've broke me off a lil' something something a long time ago on G.P. I know I ain't no bitch, but you ain't got to be scared to spoil me. Being broke is unbearable whether you up North or down South"

"Then get this paper. Maybe then you'll stop complaining about child support tearing your ass out the frame"

Shine stared at the phone like he couldn't believe what he was hearing coming out of the receiver. "Is you crazy, nigga? I ain't giving them crackers shit. Jalisa neither. She be letting that nigga have too much influence in my shorty's life. Motherfucka ain't her daddy"

Suddenly KoKo didn't like the way the conversation was heading, so he pretended the reception on his cell phone was fucking up. "You still there, Shine? Can you hear me? Okay, yeah, shit straight now"

"Damn where you at? Under a bridge?"

"As a matter of fact I'm in a strip club. Bitches got so much electricity in they bodies, they phat ass and juicy titties be

25

giving off sparks, energy so hot it be fucking with a nigga's cell phone.

"Put one of them hoes on, let me holla -------"

"C'mon, man, fuck these mud ducks. What about the arrangement I was kicking a minute ago? A second ago, your ass was ready to make love to them digits I throwed at you?

"The numbers lovely, it's the goddamn aftermath that I ain't wanting to deal with"

"But you can do it"

"Of course, you would say some foul shit like that. Family must not count for nuthin' in the 21st century 'cause it damn sho' look like you trying to get me played right out of my life"

"You can do it, Shine" KoKo pleaded. "Handle that"

"How the fuck I'm supposed to trick a motherfucka into thinking I'm a real thug. I'm a school-boy, not a gangsta and a true thug like that thug Rah-Rah who the face of Harlem's crime syndicate will peep my shit in a heart-beat. Then what? No mo' motherfucking Shine, that's what and personally cuz, I feel much too strongly about pussy and weed to be getting wet up over a beef that I ain't got nuthin' to do with"

"A 100 grand can buy a lot of ass and grass"

"But bullets hurt, cuz. That's the damn point I'm trying to make and I'm to young to consider suicide -------"

"You did when you brought up that silly bullshit about trying to fake Rah-Rah out like I'm some big, bad gangsta. I'm Mr. 9-5 and that nigga Murder Incorporated. You get the picture?"

"Look Shine, I'll school you"

That made Shine laugh so hard snot flew out of his nose. "Is this gonna be like one of those long distance courses where you get your degree by mail" Shine laughed some more. "What you gonna teach me, how to freak a Black & Mild?"

"Now, you wanna get stupid on me. If I was in the mood for stupid, I'd be stuck up under one of these dizzy half-naked dames in this hole-in-the-wall, but I'm trying to put some money in your pocket"

"So what I'm supposed to do, just roll up on Rah and pretend I'm some big baller who wanna help him wipe out y'all rooty-toot country boys?"

"Like I said, you'll be well schooled"

"Nigga, call me back. I need to sort shit out"

Shine couldn't sit still. Eventhough he did not welcome the chance to fuck with that nigga Rah-Rah he did possess a total fondness for all the luxuries 100g's could buy, and under any other circumstances he would kiss the motherfucka's ass that lined up a shot for some grand prize money like what his cousin was kicking, but a goddamn bullet to the head had a way of spoiling all the fun. Without a doubt Rah was not to be fooled with. Nigga was like Mother Nature, wasn't nice to fuck with.

But being broke was a different issue. Something Shine was on intimate terms with and he despised that bitch Poverty, but she was hard to shake.

Shine was so broke right now, he was almost convinced that if a motherfucka looked at the dollar sign closely enough, you could see his black ass on it. There he would be nailed to the sign like Jesus had been crucified on the cross.

Fuck Rah-Rah!

There were rumors that a top clothing store uptown had just got a fresh shipment of new gators in. Shine rubbed his bare feet. A funky pair of gators would put a whole lot of pep in his step. And he didn't see a damn thing wrong with a couple of pair of lizards, about 3 sets of snakes -----Anaconda was the shit -----and he had to cop him some crocodiles. Shine laughed. His motherfucking closet would have so many reptiles in it, he'd have to hire Steve Irwin, that crazy white dude from the Crocodile Hunter, to come to his crib and tame his footwear.

Firing up his incense burner, Shine already felt fabulously wealthy and fucking with crazy ass Rah-Rah somehow didn't seem so crazy after all. He couldn't wait on KoKo to call back.

On his journey through the open floor of the club, dancers placed small bets on who could trap him off, but KoKo brushed the bitches off until he was approached by a cutie-pie who looked underage but who had titties and ass bigger than any of the bootylicious vets that decorated the spot. The young bitch had her 'do' done up with plum highlights that made her whole head sparkle like the hair fairy had flossed her shit with star dust. Sista wore gold hoop earrings and a pale yellow off-the-shoulder dress by Tom Ford, both of which made a wonderful contrast to her dark skin tone. The bitch ----- whoever she was ------- was up and coming, a future somebody if she didn't let these niggas drag her through the mud and scandalize her name.

She approached gracefully and suddenly KoKo was concerned about what he was going to say to her. Then the young lady fell apart, giggling like a schoolgirl.

"I had your ass, KoKo," she laughed. "Had your damn tongue hanging out of your mouth like a dog" She spun around. "Admit it, nigga, I am fly, ain't I?"

"Janeen, girl, what the fuck your little young, fast ass doing up in heah. How old you anyway? Fifteen?"

"Really my age don't concern you"

"It do if the police bust up in heah"

"Nigga, pleeze. Your trifling ass wasn't concerned about how old I was before you recognized me. Bet you would've fucked me. I shouldn't have said shit and let you hit on me, so I could've told Kendra"

"Wouldn't nuthin' have happened 'cept you would have gotten the shit slapped out of your sister if she would've come at me with some bullshit your ass done tole her" KoKo signed. "Anyway, fuck that. What are you doing up in Champagne's?"

"You a writer or a playa?" Janeen huffed. "Hard to tell with you all up in my biz'ness, but just in case you writing a damn book, please spell my damn name right"

KoKo shook his head. "I know I done said it before, but you the most fast-assed young hussy I ever seen in my life.,"

"Then your ass should feel blessed"

"Why?"

"Why?!", Janeen sounded pained. "Why?! Playa, how many times in a lifetime do a nigga see the total eclipse of the sun? One, if his ass lucky. What about a goddamn falling star? Once, if that. And hear your dumb ass is seeing me with my gorgeous self all the time and got the nerve not to know how blessed you are. It's motherfuckas in the graveyard right now that didn't get the chance in their lifetime to behold such beauty as I possess" Janeen patted her hair, smacking her lips. "I should slap your face"

KoKo laughed loudly. "Come on, I'll buy you a drink -- ----- of orange juice"

"No the hell you won't neither" Janeen stopped dead in her tracks. "I wanna sip the real shit"

"Orange juice or nuthin', Janeen"

"How the fuck it gonna look," Janeen pouted, "for a ho with all my realness to be sitting at the damn bar with a glass of goddamn kiddie juice. Why you think this joint called Champagne? That's what real bitches supposed to be getting they drank on with up in heah, but your jive ass don't hear me though. Don't let me find out you drink O.J., nigga"

"C'mon, sweet thang. Put your arm in mine"

Koko led Janeen to a row of reserved tables on a raised platform and had a seat across from her.

"Point out one bitch in heah who finer than me"

"You it, Miss Thang. You the star, but don't never think for one second that you finer than Kendra. You can't even wear your sister's panties" KoKo laughed, he was feeling good. "You still ain't tole me -------"

"Damn, you nosy. Anyway, my man on lock so I gotta get a job to hold it down for us. I get me a job dancing and I can keep his commissary phat to death"

KoKo nodded his approval. "You get big ups for that, young sista. For a fifteen -------"

"Sixteen"

"I ain't got nuthin' but mad respect for a sixteen year old sista who down with her man like that, but it's 'bout mo' than sending a motherfucka money while he on lockdown. It's also about keeping your legs closed until the nigga raise up. I know it might get hard when a bitch get hot in the ass, but that don't mean she gotta be slanging pussy out of both draw legs. You feel me?"

Janeen nodded demurely. "My man ain't got but a year. I think I can make it without being some other nigga's mistress. I wanna represent for my Boo"

"Yep, girl, you ane Kendra's sister a'ight. Miss Iris raised both of y'all and I'm glad as hell that I got me one of y'all"

"Ain't no man in the world can handle both of us"

KoKo smiled slyly. "I don't know 'bout that, but I do know that there ain't no man, me included, that deserves both of y'all" He grabbed Janeen's hands and kissed it. "You and Kendra special. For real"

It was well past midnight when KoKo remembered he had to hit Shine back. He punched the digits out.

"In or out?" KoKo asked.

"Nigga, stack my paper"

"Good looking, cuz"

"When I get paid?"

"I'll send everything up with your teacher"

"Who that?"

"She'll be there Sunday"

"She?!"

"Don't get no funny ideas. It's K., my peeps. But hold on" KoKo stared across the table at Janeen. "Nigga, I'm gonna make you love me 'cause I'm gonna send a young sista up there who so fine you'll get a nut just looking at her"

"Who she look like, Alicia Keys?"

"Nope"

"Ashanti?"

"No"

"Well, who then?"

"She sitting right across from me. Holla at her. Her name Janeen. Ask her who she look like. KoKo handed the phone across the table"

"Nigga, don't be asking no other nigga how I be looking" Janeen scolded Shine, " 'cause how he gonna tell your ass when the dictionary ain't even got no words to describe how goddamn drop dead gorgeous I am"

"You got butt?"

"Like a government mule"

"Titties?"

"Look like I got two footballs stuffed under my blouse"

"Put my cuz back on. Hurry up"

Janeen returned the phone to KoKo.

31

"What's up?"

"Make sho' that honey pack plenty of thongs"

Chapter 4

Kendra didn't say a word. Instead she threw herself into Shine's arms and held onto him like he was an A-list celebrity. She kissed him on the lips and was hanging all over him as if she would never let him go. Even Janeen got in the act. Hugging, squeezing and kissing Shine until he was breathless.

"That's enough," Kendra said coldly. "You never know who's watching. Now let's go" She glared at Shine over the top of her dark designer sunglasses. "If you're gonna serve them niggas, you definitely gonna need some gear. That shit you playing played out"

"Word" Janeen asked flippantly. "That shit wack"

"Damn", Shine cursed, "Who y'all, the wicked witches of the South?"

"Put our bags in the car and let's go"

Shine shook his head. "Not until I see my paper"

Kendra leaned over as though she was going to kiss Shine, but abruptly grabbed him in the collar. "Now be honest. You wouldn't really prefer me opening up a briefcase with 100 grand in it right out here in front of the airport, now would you?"

Shine looked around nervously, and considered the possibility of being robbed. "Naw. I'll wait"

"That's what I thought", Kendra smiled sweetly. "Now, load our bags in the damn taxi like I told you"

Janeen touched her sister's arm. "And make the nigga put his eyes back in his head"

Kendra and Janeen had arrived in New York just as the Apollo Theater was preparing to celebrate its 70th anniversary. Kendra would have loved being in attendance at the star-studded gala which would air on NBC with Denzel Washington opening the show, but she would be reluctant to step out that early with Shine. The nigga was too green and would more than likely do something to embarrass himself. And her.

During the cab ride to the hotel suite, she and her sister would 'occupy'. Kendra understood how important this was to KoKo and she was determined to pull Shine through his ordeal, but she had to keep the brotha focused. Already, she had been quick to notice how he had been mesmerized by Janeen and that made her angry because this was not a booty call although she knew Janeen would flaunt her ample assets, dizzying the nigga up and leaving him pussy drunk.

At the hotel, Kendra pointed to a suitcase. "That one yours," she informed Shine, her voice showing no emotion. "We'll take you shopping because in order for this to come off right, you gotta look the part. Kendra walked towards Shine, examining him like he was a lab specimen. After a second, she glanced away, her mind making calculations and deductions. "You got the look", she whispered thoughtfully. "I like the bald head, but gotta thug up your mug -------"

"Ain't shit wrong with my goddamn face the way it is, is it, cutie-pie?" Shine smiled for Janeen.

"What she think or says don't mean a damn thang and let me get something straight right now. She's here to work with you, not work out on your dick" Kendra looked at Shine, then at her sister. "Both of y'all got that?"

"Girl, I got a man at home" Janeen turned up her nose. "Plus they say it's a lot of niggas up here on the DL"

Kendra watched Shinbe for his reaction. Then she quizzed Janeen. "So you think homeboy could be creeping on the Down Low?"

Janeen put her hands on her hips. "The thought has crossed my mind. Word on the street is that brothas up in the Apple like worms, if you catch my drift"

Kendra exploded. "Nigga! Here go a bitch telling you to your face that you might be pussy and you standing there like it's all good" Kendra got up in Shine's face. "By law, you supposed to slap the cow-walking shit out of a ho that question your manhood. Real niggas sensitive about that 'cause they manhood and they word the shit they use to build they rep on" She pushed Shine in his chest. "If either a man or a woman go south on you 'bout your sexual preference, you get religious on they motherfucking stank ass and nigga do you know what your religion is? The goddamn gun. Every thug belong to The Church of the Glock" Kendra relaxed. "Don't forget that!"

Shine tilted his head back and lifted his eyes up to the ceiling.

"Don't even go there. I'm all the help you gonna get so leave Jesus alone"

"So how long this shit gonna last?"

"As long as it takes to get your square ass in order"

"What part of New York you from anyway?" Janeen snapped. "I thought all New York brothas were cool and had it going on. You must be from Upstate"

"I'm from Virginia Beach, in V.A., if you gotta know"

Janeen frowned up her face in revulsion. "No wonder you ain't no motherfucking thug. Virginia Beach? Niggas down there will grab a guitar 'fore they grab a gat"

"Them guitars and shit you dissing is what got the Neptunes, Timbaland, Magoo and them paid in full"

"Okay, okay, you two. Enough of that bullshit. Now, back to what I was saying. You need to thug up your look, you know, grow something to add on to that lil' weak-assed mustache. A beard will accent your bald head especially when it's precision trimmed" When Kendra saw the smirk on Shine's face, she smacked her lips. "You got something on your chest you feel like you need to get off?"

"Why don't I just stick a bone through my motherfucking nose or won't that be enough to command respect?"

"Brotha, you pathetic"

"Let you tell it"

Kendra laughed. "A bitch like this," she pointed to Janeen, "will trick you out of every damn dollar in that suitcase and have your silly ass down in the welfare line within a week. A gold digging ho is a thousand times more devious -------"

"Bitch can't get shit from me but good dick"

Both Kendra and Janeen laughed.

"I bet you ain't never called a woman a bitch to her face"

"Do I gotta call my cuz to get y'all out of my private life? This ain't about turning me into no pimp. I ain't gotta confront Bishop Don Magic Juan"

36

"True, my brotha, you ain't, but what you fail to see is that a thug can't possess no kind of cool or self-assurance if he pussy-whupped"

"So a nigga a sucka if he in love?"

"I ain't saying that, but it can be dangerous. You see, in the game the two niggas most suspect are the dope-fiend and the pussy-whupped. Either of 'em go to jail and ain't no telling how they might show. A dope-fiend be worrying 'bout his get high and the nigga who's too much in love be worried 'bout somebody fucking his woman. One scared the dope man gonna slang up all the dope while he gone and the other motherfucka scared his woman gonna be slanging ass and then guess what's gonna happen. Sucka be beating on the cell door, yelling for the jailer to go get the D.A. so he can snitch"

"That's crazy"

"It is. How?"

"How? How a motherfucka gonna be halfway in love or a little bit into his feelings. He either in love or he ain't"

Kendra scowled. "You got a good point, but a real thug, without even knowing how he does it, can put brakes on his love so he don't get caught up 'cause if he do it's a weakness the police can use against him, so a thug despises a pussy-whupped nigga worst than a dope-fiend"

"And that's why you gotta step to a ho who tries to diss you," Janeen added. "If you can't control a women, how you gonna control an empire?"

Shine scratched his bald head. "What y'all run down there, thug school?"

Kendra smiled. "Our Mama raised us well. We know how to service our men without being in the way, but that ain't none of your biz'ness. Your suite ----------"

"Suite? I got a motherfucking crib"

"It ain't worthy, so now you living heah until we see fit to cut your ass loose. We go shopping at one"

"Don't forget we gotta leave him some time to watch the videos"

"Videos? What videos?"

Kendra thought for a moment. "Where they at?"

"In one of my bags"

"Give 'em to him"

"What videos?!" Shine asked once more.

"Sugar Hill, New Jack City, Scarface. Pay attention to the lead figures so you can copy some of their mannerisms"

"But them niggas was acting"

"Like that ain't what you gonna be doing"

"Damn" Shine cursed.

"Damn, my ass. Them videos part of your study plans"

Janeen giggled. "I'll watch them with you"

Kendra rolled her eyes. "I don't think so"

Shine sighed. "Can I at least go back to the hood to pick up my ride?"

"You won't need it. So put it in storage. KoKo gonna let you borrow one of his whips. He's having it shipped up. Should arrive tomorrow"

"Wh-what is it?"

"You'll find out when it gets here"

Janeen put her hands on her hips. "If it's what I think it is, I'm driving that bitch and I don't give a damn what neither of y'all say"

"Girl, you a trip"

Shine laughed. "That's what I was thinking about both of y'all. Both of y'all tripping, but it just might be a trip I enjoy" He eyeballed Janeen down. "You feel me?"

38

Meanwhile.

The U.S. District Court of The Southern District of New York was home to one of the most vicious prosecutors in the country and Rah-Rah couldn't stand her ass. The bitch was intelligent and ambitious and had climbed up the political ladder on the backs of niggas she had convicted and put away for long prison bids. Many of Rah-Rah's soldiers had fallen victim to the cruel brand of white justice.

Now, he was back in court again. This morning they were bringing two of his boys for arraignment. The DEA had snatched both of them up and had charged them with conspiracy to commit murder. It was, by now, also common knowledge that the prosecutor, Pamela Harrington, was going to slap them with a drug conspiracy charge.

Rah-Rah pondered the ways of the judicial system and concluded that it was not geared to work in the interests of urban youth. Rah-Rah gritted his teeth at that chilling conclusion and though the reality outraged him there wasn't nothing he could do about it except to avoid getting busted.

Rah-Rah had chosen today to educate his ten year old son to the world of "muck and slime" as his father had called the courthouse. Rah-Rah would not break with this family tradition because Rah-Rah Sr. had prophesied before his death that knowing the ways of the devil offered the only way to escape him, and Rah-Rah damn sure wanted Rah-Rah III to learn this lesson well.

Throwing up the sign of their Harlem set when they brought in Kronic and Daddy O, Rah-Rah kept his son informed of everything that was going on in the courtroom. He pointed out the set-up, who was who, and explained the role of the judge.

"The criminal justice system is not an honorable profession, my son," Rah-Rah whispered. "It chews men up and then spits them out"

39

Rah-Rah III made a face so Rah-Rah knew he had made his point.

Rah-Rah especially zeroed in on the prosecutor, carefully explaining that the white bitch was an ambassador for The Bureau of Prisons and that it was due to her and the strategies of her colleagues that 790,000 black men were on lockdown in this country.

When the proceedings were over Rah-Rah started to complain to the lawyers that their defense wasn't shit, but what good would it do? He threw up his set as the marshals escorted Kronic and Daddy O from the courtroom, their shackles sounding the chain-gang shuffle. Then he was alone with Rah 3.

Standing outside in the corridor, Rah-Rah stooped down to look his shorty in the eyes. "Don't ever forget what you saw this morning, Rah 3, 'cause it's important. Don't ever let the white man put chains on you because once he does, you'll always be his slave. Don't ever forget that once they get you in their courtroom that you done for. The judge ain't got no love for you. The D.A. Ain't got no love for you, and your own goddamn lawyers ain't nuthin' but blubbering fools until you hit the right dollar amount. Then and only then will they try to get you out of danger"

"What they gonna do with your friends?"

"Judge denied bond in their case which means that with all my paper I can't get 'em out of jail. They good people so they will soldier on until the bitter end"

On the ride back to Harlem, a big part of Rah-Rah's proclamation to Rah 3 was that America, as a whole, didn't matter to them. Their nation was the hood and they owned patriotism only to the block which they had a duty to protect and defend with their lives. Any nigga who wasn't willing to die for his hood was a coward, and right on the spot he took an oath from Rah 3 to never tolerate an insult to the block because it was a slap in the face of family and friends.

"We can never be content, Rah 3 since our family is the First Family of the hood. Much of our family blood, dating back to your great-grandfather, was shed to establish the mad props we be getting today. And to keep our position strong and our set tight, we gonna have to honor our turf. It's sacred ground, Rah 3, because a lot of the blood and bones our thug ancestors buried there. You let an outsider tread on your sacred ground and it just like the nigga done raped your Mama or spit in your face"

When they rode past 110th Street Rah-Rah's eyes grew misty. "This is your country, Rah 3. Fuck America. You belong to the nation of Harlem" He stepped on the gas and then he rolled down 125th Street. "That's your landmark" He pointed at the Apollo Theater. "The crackers got the Washington Monument, The White House, Grant's Tomb, but this is ours. Do you know how many of our great entertainers have come across the Apollo stage?"

Rah 3 shook his head. "No sir"

"Man," Rah-Rah said wistfully. "Man, you got the old school legends"

"Like who?"

"Like who?" Rah-Rah commented playfully. "Well, let's see. You had Lady Day, Ella Fitzgerald, Sarah Vaughn, Sammy Davis Jr., Nancy Wilson. Then you had great people like Aretha Franklin, James Brown, Nat King Cole," Rah-Rah laughed. "Even brothas like Redd Foxx and Richard Pryor paid their dues on the 125. A motherfucka diss Harlem, he dissing black history" Rah-Rah signed. "A nigga's block is his heritage and though ain't no other niggas on the planet that carry the historic legacy that we do, niggas still gotta throw up they set, gotta represent 100%. You understand?"

Rah 3 said he did.

Chapter 5

The Chrysler 300C was bling-bling on wheels! It glistened in front of the hotel like the chariot Zeus pushed when he charged through the sky of Olympus. The whip was blistered with so much attitude and flash that Shine couldn't make up his mind whether to take pictures of the fly motherfucka or to jump in and speed off, leaving Kendra and Janeen's asses standing there with their mouths hanging open.

Shine dangled the keys. "I should make y'all walk. Some pleasures are meant to be enjoyed alone"

"Nigga, pleeze," Janeen shrieked as she and Kendra piled in the sumptuous interior of the car. "This bitch smell showroom fresh. Damn!"

Even Kendra was visibly impressed, but in her role as the Supercool Madam she kept her comments to herself; however the royal aura of the 300C caused her senses to exhilarate with rip-roaring vigor. The chrome trim on the door handles, the cup holders, the detailing around the control knobs and the push-push doors for the ashtray almost warped her mind. This whip was way it!

"Oh shit, it just hit my ass," Janeen yelped excitedly. "This the whip from out of the 50's video. No goddamn wonder I knew I had seen a ride like this before. I love that video and now here I am sitting on twenty-twos in one just like the one that be funking with 50" Janeen smiled brightly. "We so on the scene!"

"Where cuz get this from?"

"Don't know," Kendra huffed. "Musta just got it. First time I done seen it"

Driving through Manhattan, Shine felt the 300C melt into his flesh and veins, reinventing him. At once, he felt like a real baller and he was so caught up in the illusion that he was rocked by a powerful jolt of gangsta rapture.

"Bitch", he snarled at Kendra, "don't just sit there. Put in a CD"

Kendra was shocked. She craned her neck like a mad cobra. "Excuse me, but evidently something wrong with the acoustics in this car 'cause I know you ain't said what I just thought you said"

"Ain't shit wrong with the sound in this car, 'cept ain't none coming out them motherfucking speakers" Shine glanced over at Kendra. "And hell yeah, I called you bitch ------- right to your face. Bitch!"

Janeen broke out in hysterical laughter. "Pimp on, playa-playa. It's your thang"

"True dat," Shine confessed. "I'm feeling so real right now that I'm gonna take y'all hoes to dine at The Crab Inn"

"If your bald-headed ass live that long," Kendra cracked. "Let this damn car change you if you want to, nigga. I don't know what the hell happening to your ass"

"Well I do"

"Me too," Janeen giggled.

"And since you the only somebody up in heah that's uninitiated," Shine lectured, "let me tell you a lil' story about butterflies. You see, they wack until they get up in they cocoon. Then they experience some shit called metamorphosis and then they motherfuckas butterflies whereas before they was caterpillars"

"So what he trying to say," Janeen added, "is that this flyassed 300C is his cocoon" She touched Shine on his shoulder. "Do I see right or what, my brotha?"

"You see, young beautiful sista, you see. You blessed with 20/20 playa vision. You know one when you see one. Now, as for your big sista sitting up front, I think she needs a pair of bifocals 'cause she seeing crooked"

"Is that so?" Kendra mumbled.

"Sho' is and if you start some shit thinking I'm the same ol' nigga, I just might pimp slap your silly ass"

"What you gonna put in the CD?", Janeen asked before Kendra could respond.

"Some Crunk. That's the only kind of music worthy of breaking these speakers in, so hand me that Lil' Jon. We getting ready to crank up the Crunk" He touched Kendra's leg. "By the way, do you know what crunk means?"

"Hell no"

"Crazy Real Urban Nigga Kings!"

To add to the tension, Shine demanded that Kendra stay in a bitch's place, keep her goddamn mouth shut, and to let him choose his own motherfucking gear.

At the Armani Exchange on Fifth Avenue and 51st Street, Shine strolled in like he owned the joint. He walked in the middle of the store, stretched forth his arms like Charleston

Heston did as Moses in The 10 Commandments and shouted. "Do me! Take these broken wings, I beg you, and drape them with the illest shit you have to offer a playa"

Kendra rolled her eyes. "That's how people act at the zoo"

"Well, then, just consider me a 6 feet, bald-headed, blue-black lion"

"With a gold tooth," Janeen added.

"And a big, ol' dick," Shine concluded, grabbing his crotch.

Kendra stomped her foot. "You on your own nigga, but if you buy some sucka shit, I'm gonna make you put it back, you understand?"

"Honey, this The Armani Exchange. I doubt very seriously if they got any sucka shit up in heah"

Kendra looked around her at all the magnificent clothing surrounding her. "Yeah, you got me there, nigga. Probably ain't no sucka shit in heah, but there damn sho' a sucka in the store. You"

"Go 'head on, sista, with that funky-assed 'tude. I'm gonna feed your ass in a minute. Sistas get evil when they hungry. My bad"

Kendra stormed off.

Shine shopped 'til he damn near dropped. After The Armani Exchange, he hit Macy's, then The Gucci Shop, followed by Prada.

"You shop like a bitch," Kendra snapped breezily. "All that fucking shit"

"Don't hate me 'cause I'm a butterfly"

Janeen helped carry the bags. "This nigga got Prada, he got Gucci, Armani. Nigga got Polo, Sean John, and Versace"

"And no goddamn sense" Kendra eyed the gear. "If you think clothes gonna elevate you to another level, you out of your mind. You might can talk the talk, brotha, but can you walk the walk?"

Shine bowed before Kendra. "That, my Nubian Queen, is a difficulty I pray I'll overcome with your illustrious assistance" Shine raised himself up and gathered the two sisters around him. "Now, let us go consume ourselves in what I'm told is one of the most spectacular dining experiences in all of Manhattan"

"Where are we going? Janeen wanted to know. "The Crab Inn"

"No ma'am, we ain't. We going to One Fish Two Fish"

That night -------- at ten -------- Kendra summoned Shine to her suite and as soon as he had entered he noticed the theater equipment was set up. His expression hardened because he was not practically in the mood to view no old-assed gangsta flicks from the 70's, but when he saw how Janeen couldn't stop giggling, he instantly got the impression that something else might be coming.

"What's on the agenda tonight?", he snorted.

"Strip down to your underwear"

"I beg your motherfucking pardon. Do the fuck what?"

Kendra pulled an instrument out of a bag that resembled a flashlight and tossed it in a chair. "Get almost naked. Just keep your draws on"

"For what?"

Janeen giggled.

"I don't see neither one of y'all coming out of y'all clothes, so what up, Kendra? You gonna let me do your sister while you video it"

"Nigga, pleeze," Janeen gasped. "You ain't never getting none of this"

"You know you want me to greet that pussy, girl"

"You gonna do like I instructed your ass or not?"

"So now all of a sudden, you a goddamn instructor. Plus ain't nuthin' coming off 'til I get the run-down"

"This is an experiment," Kendra sighed. "I think it's time we solved the problem of you being weak for women"

"And I gotta get naked?"

"Just do it", Janeen pleaded, "so we can get it over with and then go out to a strip club"

"A strip club?!" Shine's eyes lit up. "Which one?"

"Ain't going nowhere until we finish this"

"You a female Pharoah," Shine groaned, undressing.

Kendra smiled slightly. "Now that you done made the decision to cooperate, I'll put you down. Sit there" Kendra nodded at her sister. "The lights, please"

"Damn" Shine croaked, "y'all scaring me with all this suspense. If ya'll gonna whup me, just pull out the whips and chains and get busy, but all this melodramatic shit -----------"

"Shut up, nigga"

"You too, Janeen. I thought me and you was on the good foot?"

When the screen flashed bright, Kendra cleared her throat.

"What you are about to see is Triple X pornography"

"Yikes!" Shine exclaimed. "Porno?"

"Shut up and listen" Kendra grabbed the flashlight-looking thing. "See this?"

"What the fuck is it?"

"An electric prod"

"A what?!"

"A prod and it carries more than a little bit of juice"

"Not enough volts to kill you," Janeen chimed merrily, "but enough so you'll get the message"

"Now the deal ----------------"

"Deal?!", Shine yelled. "What kind of goddamn deal is it when you fixing to electrocute a nigga?"

"Don't start acting like a ho, please. If lil' ol' bitty rats in a maze can handle it, a grown-assed man shouldn't have no problem"

"You sick, sista. Something bad wrong wit' you"

"Anyway, anytime your dick gets hard while you viewing this film, I'm gonna stick your ass"

"If this don't take the cake. You gonna make me watch motherfuckas fucking and then your evil ass gonna give me a shock treatment if I get aroused. What kind of foolishness is that, giving a nigga a test he can't pass? Like I said, if you wanna punish me, go 'head on and snatch out your whips and chains. Rather that, than this"

"As I was going to say," Kendra remarked calmly. "It's all in your mind. You gotta learn to control your dick. Just because you see pussy ain't no call for your dick to get hard"

"Since when?"

"Since your ass wanted to become a playa, that's when. Anyway, the trick is to remind yourself not to get turned the fuck on. These are total strangers. The bitch ain't offering you no ass. She at work, no different from the bitches at a car wash. Do a bitch washing your ride get you off?" Kendra shrugged, holding up the prod. "Never mind, that's what mama's little helper is for" She laughed. "Shall we begin?"

49

Being a cold-bloodied square Shine hadn't been blessed with many occasions to step out on the town with a woman as exquisite as Kendra. Sista was a bonafide dime, an arm trophy 100% guaranteed to increase a mothefucka's status.

Looking her over (almost greedily) Shine found himself smiling (and lusting), but Kendra's worth as a woman was priceless, an inspiration to mankind. She looked only a tiny bit taller in her strap-on heels, but the added height brought the top of her head to just under his chin.

Shine was puzzled by how the Creator, in all his infinite wisdom, had come up with the shade of black he had favored for Kendra's skin tone. It radiated; glowed. And those eyes? It was easy for him to believe that, with the minor exception of Janeen, no one else in the universe had peepers like hers. They twinkled like jewels, twin windows to the world.

Being wise enough not to pay too much attention to her body he was convinced though, that nothing she had under her Gucci gown needed improvement.

In the suite, Janeen was still pitching a bitch because Kendra wasn't going to let her go with them to Lone Leg Up, a bawdy sex club that specialized in orgies.

"I just want to go to satisfy my curiosity," Janeen yelled. "I'm a woman so why can't I go?"

"One Leg Up is ---------"

"Damn, Kendra" Shine protested, "she just sat through a Triple X porn video"

"That was for educational purposes. Plus who the fuck you? I don't want her in no spot where there is live sex and this discussion is over. And if I were you, my brotha, I would be thinking about my own conduct. Your sorry ass failed the video test. How you gonna come through when the action is live. Mama's little helper up"

On the up and up One Leg Up didn't exist as a place of its own. What it was, more precisely, was Palagia, the female founder, who sponsored orgies at real locations scattered throughout Manhattan. One week the sexual hi-jinks might take place in a loft at Tribeca, the next week on location at a HBO reality show. Tonight, however, the action was jumping off on East Houston Street at a bar called Carnaval.

Kendra and Shine arrived fashionably late, but early enough to get their bearings before the after midnight gong sounded which was a signal for everybody in the joint to get naked and to get busy.

Once Kendra had whispered the password into the ear of the doorman, she and Shine were ushered inside and on the spot Shine's face grew bright with anticipation. Kendra withdrew the electric prod and dangled it in front of his face.

"Think with this head," she admonished, nudging his temple gently. "And not this one" She felt his dick. Instantly, it stiffened. "This one's on the house. C'mon", she hissed. "It's gonna be a long night. I can see that already"

The spot was filled with bitches! And being the veteran pussy-fiend he was, Shine's sensitive nose immediately sniffed out the exotic whiff of pussy and sexual exploration. He felt right at home. Kendra touched him on the arm and her mouth soundlessly formed the word THINK. "Yeah, right" he mouthed back.

Gripping Shine's arm, Kendra shouted over the music. "Nigga, this ain't no game. A lot is riding on you and if you let your dick blow it, then you lose it so fuck up if you dare"

Shine pulled away. "If I didn't know any better, I'd say you sound jealous"

"Fuck you nigga"

Shine walked off. He had to get away from Kendra. Her presence was too captivating and it brought him immense pleasure just to stand in her company so he had to lose himself in the crowd until his lust passed. When he stopped and looked back, she was still standing in the same spot, but only now it appeared as though the whole world was revolving around her. Shine felt like running, but no matter how fast or how far he jetted, he would never be able to outrun the scent of her perfume.

"I'll be back," he yelled. "Go to the bar"

Upstairs, Shine stumbled into a private orgy where a bleached blonde begged him to join them. He considered the invitation, rejected it, but when he saw the woman fall on her back and spread her legs, free white pussy caused him to toss caution to the wind.

"What would please you?", the woman purred as she raised up just enough to unzip Shine's pants. When his dick was out, the woman kissed it. "You should never cage such a lovely beast"

Another woman unbuckled Shine's belt and helped him out of his clothes. "I prefer to see the human body in all its magnificence" The woman kissed Shine on his lips then wrapped her arms around his neck. Suddenly, he could feel the other woman's lips licking his upper thighs, then he experienced the intense sensation of having his dick being slurped into a silky vortex of warmth and wetness.

Soon, a third and then a fourth woman joined Shine and his two new friends. They gently lowered his naked body to the thick carpet, promising to fulfill all his carnal desires.

One of the women covered Shine's eyes with a black, silk mask and commanded that he not struggle against the pleasure he was about to receive. He promised that nothing on earth would make him put up any resistance, and as a gift for his willing submission and surrender, one of the beautiful women -------- he didn't know which one -------- straddled his waist and slid down on his dick with such control in her pussy that he could feel her vaginal muscles squeezing and gripping his dick as if it was being bronzed. He almost screamed out in joy.

Eventhough he could feel the other women performing sexual magic with their lips on other parts of his body, his prime pleasure came from the woman riding his dick. White bitch knew how to fuck, but just as soon as he sensed he had established a close familiarity with the velvety warmth of her pussy, another one of the bitches took her place. The switch was as perfect as a passed baton in a relay race at the Summer Olympics, but his bitch was not a copy-cat. She had her own bag of tricks and the first thing she did was to bounce up and down on his dick a few times and then shifted her center of gravity so that her insides opened like a flower and he slid so far up in her that he screamed in ecstasy. He had never been that deep in a pussy before and as he explored the virgin territory, he muttered a string of curse words that floated from his mouth, expressing the devil in him.

The third woman was devoted to getting fucked doggy-style and Shine saw no reason to deny her. He dutifully climbed up on this bitch's back like he was scaling Mt. Everest, but no sooner had he invaded her pussy than he felt something jabbing him in the neck. He screamed, only this time in pain.

"Goddammit, Kendra!"

"Sorry ladies, but this big dick daddy has to leave now" She pressed the electric prod into Shine's naked flesh and depressed the button, releasing the juice.

Shine yelled. "Turn that goddamn thang down. Fuck around and --------"

"You coming or not?"

Smiling sheepishly, Shine thanked the women, wondering which one he'd missed.

"I'm gonna count to three"

Shine was visibly upset. "You could've waited until I got a nut" When he yanked off the mask, he lost his breath,

53

couldn't believe his eyes, thought he had to be hallucinating. "You-you ain't got no clothes on!"

Kendra smiled. "It's after 12:30, and please don't stare at my titties that way"

Seeming almost able to read Kendra's mind, Shine followed her back down to a lower level of the club where there was a huge dance floor. He traveled behind her slowly so that he could have more time to witness the delicious sway of her phat ass. By the time they had reached the center of the dance floor, Shine intuitively picked up Kendra's next signal so without a mumbling word, he snatched her into his open arms and starting dancing -------- no, grinding -------- with her.

No longer distracted by expensive clothes, Shine and Kendra's naked bodies made blissful contact, and sensing that he no longer had to disguise what he was feeling he cupped the cheeks of Kendra's ass and pulled her even tighter into his loins.

In response Kendra reached between Shine's leg, stroked his hard dick and shoved it in the tight space between her closed thighs. Then she rode up and down on it. Allowing the length of it to rub enticingly across her moist pussy lips.

When Shine couldn't take this insanely joyful teasing any longer he begged Kendra to let him enter her, to let him put his dick in her, but she hugged his neck tightly, whispering in his ear that it was forbidden.

"Enjoy this," she moaned, grinding against him with a burning sexual spirit that defied belief. "Please, let's just enjoy this"

Not wanting to be disobedient Shine gritted his teeth, closed his eyes and groaned like a wounded beast as he felt his nuts being smothered by the passion and heat that had burned like a fire between Kendra's thighs which had a firm clamp on his dick. Shine was delirious, but the sexual insanity was just beginning.

"Turn me around," Kendra cooed. "And rub your dick up and down my ass. Hurry up," she commanded in a voice choked with lust. "I want to play with myself while you do it"

Politely spinning Kendra around, Shine bent her over at the waist and with his dick in his hand, he thrust it between the dark mounds of her ass, running it from the closed crack of her butt to the open lips of her pussy.

Kendra gasped in delight as she felt Shine's dick roaming around the entrance of her wet, receptive pussy and deep in her heart she wished that he would betray their sexual trust and ram dick up in her. She was sure she would forgive his disobedience because if there was ever a moment when she would love and enjoy being a faithless slut------------ it was now!

Though she did not desire to stain her relationship with KoKo, she did want this nigga on her ass to fuck her, to let her put all of her sexual orifices at his service, and to let her squeeze some more cum out of his dick that he would become dehydrated.

Kendra stood, whispering sensual nothings to Shine. "Grind your big black dick against my phat ass while I play with my juicy pussy"

"Let me get you off"

"No" Kendra purred. "I'll do it. Just keep your dick where it is. Grind harder"

When Kendra experienced an orgasm a while later, she grew so weak in the knees that Shine had to support her. She smiled. "Thanks"

"The pleasure was all mine" He grabbed his still hard dick, beginning to stroke it aggressively.

"No!" Kendra objected.

Shine was confused. "Why?"

"Janeen"

Shine's face lit up. "Now, we're getting somewhere"

Given their sexually explicit conduct of last night, Kendra and Shine displayed hardly any discomfort in each other's company the following morning. Everything was back on a strictly biz'ness footing, their 'almost' status as fuck buddies lost, the moment never to be recaptured!

Shine was slightly bitter.

Kendra, however, was back to being Kendra and with her usual stay-one-step-ahead-of-the-devil attitude on LOUD, she scheduled Shine for a two o'clock session on weapons where he would participate in a crash course in the use of the firearms that urban thugs and gangstas were most fond of. She would also brush him up on the history of the favorite artillery of the stick-up boys: The sawed-off shotgun.

"In the matter of pieces, a thug must be well versed" Kendra lectured, "because it is the one thing they never leave home without"

Shine didn't dispute that fact.

On Thursday, from nine to noon, Kendra arranged an instructional training session so Shine could be taught how to cook cocaine and how to cut heroin. He would also be required to learn how to interpret the potency of various drugs using only the simple power of taste. Finally, he would be expected to digest drug jargon as well as to understand the drug underworld.

"Nigga, can you roll a blunt?"

Shine nodded.

"Good because smoking is a very vital ritual in the Thug Kingdom and a nigga who can't freak a Black & Mild or wrap a blunt is instantly suspect, so don't underestimate the value of that skill"

On Friday at nine, Kendra phoned KoKo.

"He ready, baby"

KoKo was pleased. "I know you done schooled that fool well"

"He ready"

Now KoKo was cautious. "How long it gonna take you to handle your biz'ness, baby, and to tie up all the loose ends?"

"I'm about it tonight"

"That quick, huh?"

"Handling it just like that, baby. Gotta get home to my Boo real quick. Mama needs some dick"

KoKo grinned. "Plenty of it heah waiting on you"

"I heard that. Bye"

Now that school was out, it was time for her to go to work.

Kendra was ready.

Work call!

Chapter 6

The neurosurgeon rushed into the emergency room as soon as he heard the Code Blue sounded over the hospital's intercom. He quickly assembled the team of doctor's that would assist him in the delicate operation and after a swift assessment to determine just where the bullet was lodged in the victim's brain, he called out loudly for a scapel.

Dr. Newman made the sign of the cross, looked down at the patient and then performed the first incision. Even under normal circumstances, such an operation would have been extremely difficult but this one was made even more dangerous due to the patient's weakened immune system which was being picked apart by AIDS but -------- bent over the man Dr. Newnan worked furiously to save him.

Two hours later when Dr. Newnan sadly approached the young, black woman seated in the waiting room, she screamed.

"No!"

"I'm sorry, ma'am, there was not much we could do. I'm sorry," Dr. Newnan apologized again.

"Oh, my God!" Jalisa screamed before collapsing into a heap on the floor.

Kendra pouted. The thought of not taking that nigga out with that single shot to the head disturbed her. She must be slipping, otherwise she should have brought that nigga instant death, should've got him done on the spot. She was overcome with anger because when she went on a death march she craved a D.O.A. in the same way a boxer hunted for a T.K.O.

Janeen tried to comfort her big sister, "It's all good, Kendra. You put in mad work"

Kendra hesitated a second, smiled faintly, then flew into a rage. "If that motherfucka would've pulled through, it would've fucked up my mission"

"No, it wouldn't because I would've took it upon myself to finish the job"

Kendra's eyes widened.

"Your battles my battles," Janeen said proudly. "We blood. I always got your back"

Embracing her young sister, Kendra thanked Janeen for her support. Kendra had always been impressed by the level of street smarts Janeen possessed and she sensed that her baby sister had also acquired the family ability to comprehend the mood of men which would grant her the luxury of being always able to beat them to the punch.

At a young age, Iris, their mother, had repeatedly warned them that to be persuasive a woman had to have more options at her disposal than good pussy. True enough, a sweet pussy could open wallets and bank accounts, their mother had preached, but only good sense could open doors. And getting in the right doors should be a bitch's chief strategy in life.

Kendra was therefore relieved to see that "Miss Iris' teachings" had not been ignored by Janeen because home economics for Miss Iris' girls were instructions on how a bitch gained enough breathing room to negotiate with niggas on her own terms and how to compel life to reveal all its secrets. Dumb bitches, Miss Iris taught, got babies. Smart bitches got babied.

Kendra exhaled. Now was probably the perfect time to spell shit out for her sister.

"Your role in this is critical because in order for me to accomplish what I got to do, you have to sell the ho a dream," Kendra paused. "The bitch is all the way street so she is constantly on the look out for game. This being on the real, you must convince her that you are legit. Up heah, motherfuckas take advantage of each other for sport and it don't help none that the police be setting up scams and reverse stings just to have some shit to do while eating motherfucking donuts"

"Don't worry, I got my part down" Janeen smiled. "I'm gonna Halle Berry this bitch to death, act my young ass off"

"Okay, I feel you. We do this and then my Boo can get to the other biz'ness that gots to be handled"

"Will it take a lot of killing to get thangs straight?"

"That I don't know," Kendra sighed, "but KoKo gotta defend his turf, gotta take a stand for the whole South"

"I don't like New York niggas nohow. Some used to go to Hawthorne with me when I was still in school. They think they too fly and that they got all the sense and they get on my last good nerve about New York being so nice they had to name it twice.

"And speaking of school --------"

"Don't. I hate that shit. After this summer I'm gonna study at home for my GED. I ace that bitch and they can kiss my phat ass"

"Well, speaking of your ass and it is phat. Runs in the family," Kendra smiled. "Ain't no shame in the game if you get down with Shine"

Janeen was silent.

"I know your man on lockdown, but we were taught to be loyal only as long as the man was holding up his end. Motherfucka come up short, that's your green light to look for greener pastures. I ain't telling you to break the rules 'cause you don't never abandon a nigga who doing a bid if he worthy, but that don't mean you ain't never gotta skeet no mo'. Remember that time when Pops went to the joint and Moms said that *as long as she discreet, a bitch can still skeet*. What she was telling us was that you didn't fuck in the same place where you cooked"

"Which meant to take the freak show on the road"

"Exactly"

"If KoKo took a fall, would you still skeet?"

"I mean I wouldn't turn into a skeet monster and be on a mission to get a nut every chance I got, but yeah, I would get my skeet on from time to time which wouldn't make me any less devoted to my Boo"

Janeen winked slyly. "You think Shine ready for one of Miss Iris daughters?"

Thinking back to that night at The One Leg Up orgy, Kendra nodded her head knowingly. "Something tells me the nigga ready"

The following day, Jalisa kept on trying to persuade herself that the young bitch sitting in her front room was bullshitting, but the ho hadn't cracked one smile yet"

"You sho you got the right address and the right Jalisa Howard"

"I'm absolutely sure," Janeen said sweetly, "so all that's left is for you to confirm who you are at our office and --------"

"Then I can claim my prizes"

"Absolutely"

"And what are they again?"

"Come on now, Miss Howard," Janeen teased playfully, "you mean you're going to work a sista like that? Make me recite that list of goodies"

"I just want to be sure I heard you right"

"Hold on while I take a deep breath" After a slight pause. "Okay, here's what you've won. First, there's a pair of AQUASWISS watches, 2 pair of Phat Farm sneakers for everyone at this address. And for the home, you will get the JVC EX-A1 DVD system, a Sony Ericsson Gameboard, a Motorola camera phone, a Toshiba SD-P5000 television" Janeen laughed. "There's more, but please may I stop now? A sista need to catch her breath"

"Not until you mention the car and the money again", Jalisa giggled.

"The car is a new 2004 Maxima"

"Money?"

"Twenty-five thousand dollars" Janeen snapped her briefcase shut. "Satisfied?"

"And you said my boyfriend entered me in this Sweepstakes?"

"No, Miss Howard, I did not say your boyfriend. Conwellington Incorporation cannot show a true interest in your private life. What I said was that Dino Baker entered your name" Janeen leaned closer and whispered softly. "Conwellington would fire my ass in a heartbeat if they thought I was too personal with any of our Sweepstakes winners. You know how damn scared white folks are about black people cheating them out of something" Janeen straightened up. "But you didn't hear that from me"

Jalisa laughed. "Girl, you ain't gotta worry about me saying shit"

"Great" Janeen stood. "Now, just one final question. Will Mr. Baker be bringing you up to our offices to claim your prizes?"

Jalisa looked at the floor, silent.

"Excuse me, but did I say something wrong?"

"No, no it's just that Mr. Baker, er, my boyfriend-------- he got killed. Funeral day after tomorrow"

"I'm so sad to hear that, Miss Howard," Janeen said consolingly. "I'm sure he went to sing with the angels"

"Now, that I'm not so sure about" Jalisa seemed to brighten. "But the living must keep on living. Right?"

"Tell you what, Miss Howard. Damn company policy. I'll drive up to our headquarters personally. Why don't you go get your things"

"What things? I'm ready right now"

"You will need some form of identification"

"I'm good to go"

"In that case," Janeen shrugged, "so am I"

Jalisa experienced a burning flash of anger when she learned she had been tricked. The Conwellington Inc. Headquarters turned out to be nothing more than an empty warehouse and rather than finding prizes, she found she was a hostage. Janeen acknowledged Jalisa's irritation by trying to mask the seriousness of the situation, but Jalisa frowned with disgust.

"You tricked me, you bitch!" she yelled. "And I bet that trifling nigga Rah-Rah put you up to it. Tell the motherfucka to get his money from Dino, dammit. I ain't got shit for his ass"

Since Kendra had not warned her to keep any secrets from the woman, Janeen decided that the best way to gain Jaslisa's trust would be to open her eyes to what was going down as soon as possible because this way it would be a lot easier for the sista to get over the semi-kidnapping and to start believing that the whole episode would benefit her greatly.

Though she sympathized with Jalisa, Janeen viewed the manner in which she had conducted herself as a source of pride. At no time had she felt like she was going to blow it. She had too much charm and was too damn clever for that. She had felt very natural in the role, and having a loaded gun in her possession for the first time made her feel extremely grownup, but it had taken a lot for her not to whip out the jammy and then bust off a clip just to celebrate because she had just turned a corner in her life, going from schoolgirl to thug bitch! She felt gangsta!

"Chill out, bitch," she yelled at Jalisa through the locked door. "My peeps will be in heah in a lil' bit and she'll fill your ears up with news your silly ass can use, so shut the fuck up 'cause it's all good"

"How the hell you figure shit all good when you done tricked me out of my home and now got my ass locked up in a warehouse storage room? At least niggas upstate get to make one free phone call," Jalisa screamed.

"Well, let me remind you that this ain't jail" Janeen clearly enjoyed her control.

"If I have a heart attack and die --------"

"Bitch!" Janeen couldn't restrain herself. She yanked the gun out of her purse and held it to the small, rectangular window for Jalisa to see. "With this motherfucka, you ain't gotta wait for no damn heart attack"

Just then Kendra walked in. "Janeen, what in the hell are you doing?"

"What it look like? I'm guarding this 'ho with my life like a real thug bitch suppose to so take five, homey, I got this heah"

"Put that piece up, girl" Kendra then looked at Jalisa. "You alright?"

"Who let the cats out!" Jalisa shrieked as she studied Kendra through the window. "What is this, Ladies' Day over at Rah-Rah's. Oh shit, I forgot. This Sunday is Mother's Day so instead of buying y'all bitches a pair of shoes or some flowers, he gives you a gat and sends you out on a motherfucking mission. How damn romantic"

Kendra held her peace. Shine had already cautioned her that Jalisa was feisty and full of fire. Now, it was clear that the nigga hadn't exaggerated. Ho had heart. Kendra just hoped she had smarts to go long with it.

"Got a deal for you," Kendra said loudly.

"A damn deal is what got my ass in the damn fix I'm in right now, so keep it. I wanna see Rah. I think I can work something out with him"

"This ain't about Rah-Rah like that"

"Let me be the judge of that. Let me holla at Rah"

Kendra signed. "I got somebody else I think you might need to holla at first"

"Who, the devil? That's who Rah-Rah's right hand man is" Jalisa walked to the back of the small room, turning her back to the door. She didn't even turn around when Janeen unlocked the door to let her visitor in.

"Hey baby," Shine said softly. "Can a nigga get a hug?"

Jalisa spun around, her mouth falling open in awe. For as long as she had known Shine she had never seen the nigga this fly. Motherfucka looked good enough to eat. Had on a pair of imported vintage cotton demin jeans topped by a burgundy short sleeve shirt by Akademiks. His two-toned shoes were so fresh that it looked as if the goddamn gators had just showed up on his doorstep this morning and begged to get on his feet. Nigga was the shit.

"Hey,why my arms still empty?"

"Because I don't see my motherfucking child-support check in 'em Jalisha snapped smartly. Why I ain't heard from your ass, that's the question? The last time we chatted, you was supposed to send me some change in the mail or did your ass forget all about that?"

Shine dropped his outstretched arms and reached into his right pocket to extract a knot of bills. He handed Jalisa a C-note.

"Nigga, you must not know what kind of morning I done had. Bitch come to my apartment, trick my ass and then lock me down like I done stole something"

Shine exhaled deeply. "I know"

Jalisa looked at the hundred dollar bill. "You sho' ain't acting like it. One Ben ain't no compensation"

"Why you gotta always talk shit 'bout everything," Shine argued. " Damn. That's the main reason I left your ass. Can't never please you, no matter what" Shine peeled off more money and stuffed the bills into Jalisa's bra. "Now, listen carefully"

Now that the situation was finally put into perspective, Jalisa looked at Kendra with renewed interests. "I was wrong about you"

"I'm just looking out for my man"

"You a down bitch. I gotta give you credit for that"

Kendra shook the compliment off. "It's like Zora Neale Hurston once said, -----"

"Zora, who?"

"Another sista. Anyway she said that black women were the mules of the world"

Jalisa nodded. "Ain't that the truth. Sistas be carrying the weight of the world on our back, but this nigga of yours. Is he worth all this? From what you yourself just said, niggas on the verge of a Thug Civil War and your man getting greedy to instigate some shit that gonna kick it into high gear"

"The war has already started. I just want to give my man an edge"

"But this is Rah-Rah he fucking with. The only edge a nigga get is not to fuck with the fool at all"

Over the last half hour, Kendra and Jalisa had sat together ------- alone -------- in the small room talking face-to-face, discussing shit sista-to-sista.

"Well, you damn sho' gonna need all the help you can get" Jalisa commented matter of factly, "but I have doubts------"

"About what?"

"My Ex"

"If that's all that troubling you," Kendra replied, "then it's no problem"

Jalisa shook her head firmly. "It would be hard for Al Capone to play Rah and you think stupid-assed Shine can do it. I just as well not put my black dress up after they bury Dino 'cause Shine's ass gonna hit the sandbox so quick it ain't gonna be funny"

Kendra pondered her options. There was no Plan B. "I'll take my chances"

"Well, get me and my babies as far away from Harlem and New York as possible 'cause if Rah-Rah figures this scheme out, which he will, I ain't wanting to be nowhere to be found" Jalisa frowned glumly. "Ever heard of a Glock headlock? It's a Rah-Rah specialty. It's where two of his goons put your head between two Glocks, one on each side, and blast. The aftermath ugly"

"I'll send you to North Carolina the same day the funeral over. You can tell Rah-Rah you can't stand to be in Harlem no mo' since Dino dead, that you gotta go"

"Ain't got to explain shit to Rah's ass. You get me the hook up and I'm gone. It's time. I'm tired of this shit. How them niggas down South do a bitch?" Jalisa laughed bitterly. "Can't nobody do me no worse than that bastard Dino. Nigga abused me and I ain't ashamed to say I'm glad he gone. At first it was a shock 'cause the fool did keep the bills paid and he provided for my babies --------"

"Now, you're gonna have your own money"

"Fifty grand?"

"Plus a new car. And now a new crib. How you feel about a three bedroom joint?"

"Oh my God! Are you for real?"

"The times are too serious not to be real, you got it coming if you introduce Shine to Rah-Rah. The rest will be on Shine"

"May Jesus be with that boy, but okay, I'll do it" Jalisa tried not to imagine what the bloody times ahead would be like as the thugs from the North and South shot it out. More than likely, it would be very terrible, a nigga Armageddon.

"Just introduce Shine as your cousin from Virginia ---"

"Oh shit!" Jalisa squealed, clamping her hands over her mouth. "I just remembered something"

"What?"

"Whitney"

"Whitney? Who's Whitney?"

"Me and Shine's daughter. Rah knows her, buys her shit for Christmas so how it gonna look if she calling Shine daddy. A lot of cousins be fucking, I guess, but I ain't even wanting to go there, trying to explain how I got a baby by my own damn cousin"

Briefly tormented by fear, Kendra suddenly hit upon a solution. "Why don't you just let me keep Whitney while you're at the funeral"

Jalisa glanced at Kendra suspiciously.

"I'm good with kids. I'll take her shopping, then we could watch a movie. Please," Kendra begged. "There's no other way. Of course, your child by Dino would have to be at the services, but it's not necessary for Whitney"

Jalisa sighed. "I guess so"

"Trust me, your daughter will have a good time with Auntie Kendra"

"And I can leave right after the funeral?"

"I promise that everything will be ready"

"The money? The car?"

"The crib. Everything"

"Okay," Jalisa whispered with finality. "I'll handle my end"

Chapter 7

Now that Dino had been laid to rest, Rah-Rah didn't care to be a part of the hugging and kissing that usually closed out most funerals because sadness and sympathy were distractions he had no use for. Dino had been a good soldier --- ---- at times ------- but the nigga was now history so Rah-Rah saw no real need to greet or meet his kin folk although he would holla at Jalisa and stick a knot in her purse for the kids.

When he spotted her hugging some middle-aged dame in a black Sunday-go-to-Meeting hat, he gave her the high sign, motioning for her to step to him. He wondered if the lady was Dino's mom and if so should he at least extend his condolences. Fuck it. For him Jalisa represented Dino and whatever feelings he had in his heart for the nigga, he would express to her.

Rah-Rah, a medium-built, brown-skinned brotha, watched impatiently as another crowd of mourners surrounded her, either pecking her on her cheeks or shaking her hand. It would be a miracle if she could get away within the next 10 minutes but catching his eye Jalisa gave him a look that said 'hold on', so Rah-Rah relaxed. Pretending to be in no hurry, he lit up a Black & mild.

Jalisa made a show of strength when she did finally approach Rah-Rah, but he knew a lot of hatred had to be running through her mind right now. Her bread-and-butter man was gone, and Rah-Rah experienced a twinge of guilt because he hadn't attempted to find out who was behind the killing, but right now was not really the time to be concerned with individual murders when a Civil War was brewing.

"Jalisa, I _____" Rah-Rah cut off the flow of words when a man stepped up and whispered quietly in her ear.

"Excuse me," the man apologized before walking away.

"That was my cousin from V.A"

"Like I was saying, 'cause Dino gone don't mean you can't get up with me if you need me. It's the least I can do for my dawg"

"Thanks" Jalisa hugged Rah-Rah warmly.

"Where his shorty at?"

Jalisa pointed. "Over there with my sister"

Rah-Rah peeled off 10 one hundred dollar bills. "A little something for the house" He squared his shoulders and was preparing to make his exit. "Remember what I told you about getting with me. Look, let me give you my number"

Jalisa waved the idea away. "That's alright, Rah, 'cause I'm leaving. Going to Chicago, got people out there"

"When you leaving?"

"Soon"

Rah-Rah stuffed some more hundred dollar bills into Jalisa's hand despite her protests.

"Take care, Jalisa" Rah-Rah turned to leave.

"Rah, wait"

"What's up?"

Jalisa took a big gulp of air. "You gave to me, now I think I have something to give you. Let's step over here" When they were completely alone, Jalisa stared Rah-Rah in his eyes. "Whether I'm supposed to or not, I know all about your beef with the South. Dino told me about it. Anyway, I know that you need to establish a stronghold somewhere in the South. At least that's what Dino said. I might can help"

"Keep talking, I'm listening"

"That guy, my cousin, who was whispering in my ear a while ago is a major figure in V.A"

"Oh yeah" Rah-Rah was interested. "What part?"

"Where Missy Elliott and Timberland from. Virginia Beach"

Rah-Rah stroked his goat-tee. "Say he a baller?"

"Might not be the number one baller but he up there"

"Why you telling me this?"

"If anybody can get your crew in V.A., it's him"

Rah-Rah liked what he was hearing. "And you think he --------"

"That's on you, Rah. All I can do is to introduce you and put in a good word for you. Cuz loves me to death though so-------- well, look he leaving out probably late tonight or in the morning. You wanna think about it some more --------"

"Ain't shit to think about, if it can work like that, I want to meet the nigga now, see what I'm saying"

"Hold up," Jalisa replied. "I'll go get him"

The mechanic told Kendra that he understood. Five hours.

Though it was close to one o'clock in the morning and she had been on the road since eight, the caffeine had Jalisa wide-eyed and alert, making her feel as if she could drive forever.

Taking a quick peek into the backseat, she smiled. Whitney and Dino Jr. were both asleep and she hoped they would sleep all the way to North Carolina so she wouldn't keep having to answer the same questions over and over again. Mama this. Mama that.

Using the car phone, Jalisa dialed her New York number but when the automated voice informed her that she had no messages, she turned her attention back to her driving. She would listen to some more music. She had turned the CD player off earlier so it wouldn't keep the children awake, but she didn't think it would bother them now that they were sleeping soundly.

The entire CD collection Janeen had given her was composed of Crunk music and though she was only vaguely familiar with most of the artists, who were all from Atlanta, she did like Bonecrusher so she put in his New CD and punched the song selector until she got to the song where Bonecrusher rapped about never being scared. Never Scared, that would be her motto from now on because with cash and a new start in North Cackalaki, she shouldn't have shit to be afraid of anymore.

And then, without warning, the Maxima exploded.

The next morning.

As the noon day sun beat down on Rah-Rah's $2 million home in Westchester County, 30 minutes from Harlem, he entertained Shine in the lavish, fully equipped bar in the game room.

Shine was impressed. "A castle fit for a king"

"We only do life once, so they key is to do it right from the first time, see what I'm saying"

Shine agreed, "I wanna style like this before I dance with the devil"

"All things are possible for a playa"

"Yeah, but sometimes even a playa need assistance"

"One hand gotta watch another, see what I'm saying, son? You get my back, I get your back. Everything else is gravy"

Shine kept his mouth shut. He enjoyed good conversation as well as any other playa/thug, but this was not mindless chit-chat and he knew it. Rah-Rah was fishing, trying to hook him to a position and then reel him into a binding commitment. Kendra had taught him to respect Rah's intelligence and to discourse freely and openly about general topics, but not to challenge anything said unless he felt he was being tested. Then, it would be a misfortune, Kendra had said, for him not to be brutally honest.

"You know what I truly want to do?", Rah-Rah confessed. "I want to engineer the destiny of niggas who deserve a shot. Sometimes even a real thug can only achieve so much on his own"

Shine chuckled. "Tell me about it. Feel like sometimes it just ain't meant for a playa to rise to the next level"

Rah-Rah took a quick sip of his Martell Cordon Blue Cognac and then set it aside. "Easy, playa. Hold up. The next level is always there whether a nigga has paid his due or not. What happens a lot of time, my brotha, is the evil shit men do to one another, see what I'm saying? Petty motherfuckers be blocking. You and a nigga can start out on the block together teamed up, but just as soon as the crew start to recognize some come up your dawg put shit in the game, start dealing off the bottom of the deck"

"Why, I wonder?"

"Son, it's two thangs your dawg always gonna want to shoot for. Your woman and your paper" Rah-Rah waved his hands in a 'that's-just-how-it-is gesture'. "Your dawg gonna always want to fuck your main lady and to get into your stash. The graveyard offer the proof because plenty of dawgs have gone to the Promised Land behind the pussy and paper of their partner. So, now if your dawg don't play fair, what can you expect out of the rest of the Thug Kingdom?" Rah-Rah smiled. "Obstacles, that's what"

"Days gone, Rah-Rah. Days like that dead and stanking"

Rah-Rah winked. "It just so happens that I'm in a position to change that situation. I can open doors for a nigga that he would never be able to open on his own. That's right, Shine, I got the juice to fill a motherfucka's life with nothing but the best of everything. And I mean everything"

"Sign me up," Shine laughed.

"Ever heard of a white billionaire named Warren Buffet?"

"Not that I remember. What son about?"

"Son primarily pulling his peeps up, making them all multimillionaires. Warren Buffet is my idol"

"Word"

Rah-Rah refilled their glasses. "Yeah, Shine, I want to be like Warren Buffet, cat is a financial genius and he don't mind putting paper in other people's pockets"

Rah-Rah's eyes became distant. "I want to be an urban Midas, turning everything I touch into platinum and at the same time I want to be responsible for making other playas millionaires, but like I was saying Warren Buffet has probably made more men millionaires in this country than anybody else. Every year, all these people who Mr. Buffet has made rich get together for a weekend of partying and trading advice. That's what I see myself doing. Every year invite all the playas who I have made millionaires up here to let loose with champagne and bitches from all over the world"

"Sound like a plan to me. What's stopping you?"

"I have this little problem that's been testing my patience lately"

"Oh yeah, what you gonna do 'bout it?"

"Ask for your help"

Shine raised his glass in toast. "How may I assist the Midas of Harlem?"

Let's go for a drive. Let me turn you on to some sushi.

Bandit knew for a fact that Gemini was not as hardcore as his brother, but McNasty was in Reidsville doing a bid so he had no choice except to step to Gemini. It was a known fact that Gemini was strictly stuck on parties and bitches, and as a result, the turf that his crew now controlled in Atlanta had grown smaller and smaller, but that wasn't any of Bandit's biz'ness. He had bigger thangs on his mind than just the ATL. The whole southern way of life was being threatened.

"What good is any town if a nigga can't get his party on?" Gemini asked in bewilderment. "That's what I dig about this city. Nigger can party in the ATL like he ain't got no sense"

Bandit was almost tempted to reach across the table, grab Gemini in the collar, and shake him like he was a child, but rather than doing it he remained stiff, his eyes unblinking.

"This ain't about no party, Gemini. We gonna be in a war soon and KoKo need to know where you stand, whether he got your support or not"

Gemini's yellow face turned serious. "I might need time to holla at McNasty 'bout this. We might get served by them New York motherfuckas"

In his mind, Bandit cursed Gemini's weakness and more than that Bandit despised the nigga's disloyalty to the South. In truth, Bandit had never considered either Gemini or McNasty men to be reckoned with although McNasty's heart was in the right place. Gemini was a ho.

If nothing else good came out of this trip to Hotlanta at least KoKo would not go into battle thinking he had help coming from this end, but still it would be a helluva of an assist if Gemini and his crew were more predictable.

"KoKo asked me to do whatever it would take to get you in our camp, Gemini, and I'm prepared to do exactly that"

"Bullshit"

"Naw, that's for real. You throw down with us against the niggas from up top and --------"

"Suppose I wanna stick dick in ol' fine-assed Kendra? Suppose that was my demand?"

"I can't call that, Playa"

"But you just said your boy gave you a license to do what you gotta do to --------"

"Goddammit, Gemini," Bandid exploded, "why should we have to beg you to fight for your own turf?"

"Because, goddammit, the niggas ain't shooting for Atlanta. Motherfuckas ain't crazy. Hell yeah, we smoke and party and fuck bitches like whoa, but we real war dawgs when a nigga come at us. That's a fact that's known all over the world. You don't fuck with the ATL and if y'all other lil' ol' hick towns was half the shit we was, then New York wouldn't be riding your motherfucking ass like a bitch" Gemini swole up. "I roll with the ATL so until we get the heat, tell KoKo his country ass on his own. Y'all niggers better get crunk 'cause I done seen them 'Big Apple Boys' put in work before"

Bandit bowed his head in disbelief, but when he looked up his eyes were ablaze with contempt. "Y'all Atlanta niggas truly think y'all shit don't stank, be acting like 'cause this town got big skyscrapers and streets named after presidents that it ain't in The Bottom. Better wake the fuck up, y'all don't live in no separate country"

"True dat, but until your zip code like mine you gotta watch your own back"

Bandit stood. "Anything else I need to know about y'all cowards?"

"Yeah, and this is real goddamn important. You down here talking out the side of your neck, but I'm gonna give you a free pass. You got that lil' bit, homey, but if you ever try that intimidation bullshit again, I swear I'll kill you"

Bandit didn't finch. "This is all I'm gonna say and then I'm out"

"Spit it then, nigga"

"Those who are not with us are against us and if Charlotte saves the whole South, then we talking the whole South and that means Atlanta too" Bandit turned away. "I'm out"

Gemini laughed. "Yeah, nigga, you out a'ight. Out of your goddamn mind. What your joke telling ass need to do is to trade in the Pelle Pelle you got on for a clown suit"

Bandit spit on the floor of Gemini's restaurant.

"You got that dawg," Gemini snarled, "but the next time it'll be different shit coming out of your mouth. Spit, this time. Blood, the next".

Bandit felt like he had been betrayed and knew that KoKo would feel even worse, but when Bandit phoned KoKo, he got a pleasant surprise. KoKo had worked some back porch magic and had devised a suitable alternative to Gemini's treachery. KoKo felt so good that he insisted that Bandit stay on in Atlanta for a few days to get in some much needed rest and relaxation.

"Yeah, it don't surprise me at all about Gemini. Bitch nigga fronting" KoKo explained. "Word is that a bunch of Mexicans done stepped in and they the ones who in control of the drug underworld in Atlanta, so why we need them? Niggas done already lost they city"

"How you find this out"

"Thin Man, ol' gangsta. Knew my Pops. Ol' dude cool, said he would holla at Tex-Mex, the leader of the Mexico crew down there. Thin Man said that there ain't no way the Mexicans gonna get down with us, but he would work a deal where they would remain neutral, where they wouldn't help either side and they wouldn't let the niggas from up top use Atlanta as a launching pad to get at us"

"Cool, brer"

"I'm heading up to V.A. in the a.m. to set up shop so that when Shine spin them niggas down there, we can kill 'em"

Back in Manhattan, Rah-Rah and Shine were comfortably seated in a cozy tea-room on East Fifth Street not far from the Leopard Lounge. They patiently sipped organic juice at the bar while awaiting space in the sushi room. Their conversation was light, a far cry from what it had been earlier, but Shine knew that Rah-Rah was mentally clocking him, probing for the right moment to drop the bomb, to pop the question.

Following a slight delay, the two thugs were escorted upstairs to the second floor dining room with only ten tables, a sport tailor-made for either intimate or private conversation.

"I heard this spot used to be a carriage house in the 1800's where all the rich gentlemen of the city would come and dine on caviar", Rah-Rah looked around. "Joint still has an air or aristocracy"

Shine peeped around at the white stucco walls and seemed stunned that anybody would find this spot that exclusive. It was too small and confining for him and on the for real, he would have much rather had journeyed to Sylvia's. He wasn't opposed to new or different dining experiences but this shit was ridiculous.

The whole time they ate, Shine could feel Rah-Rah sizing him up, searching his face for a clue as to what he was thinking, but Shine gave him nothing because at the moment his major concern was how to strengthen his own hand. He prayed for a position that would assure him of greater success when he made his personal play. This was not all about KoKo anymore because Shine imagined the inherent financial rewards of playing both ends against the middle. Rah-Rah would have to pay dearly if we wanted a happy landing in VA because room and board was not cheap these days.

"Do you know much about history, son?"

"Enough to know that I don't never want to be a motherfucking slave"

Rah-Rah smiled. "And that's enough to let me know that we think a lot alike. I despise not being on top"

"So what you plan to do, conquer the world"

"Don't need nothing but the South," Rah-Rah said in a teasing tone.

"A lot of people from up North going back down the way, trying to reconnect with the roots"

"Naw, naw, son, I ain't talking about the South in that way. The people that go back for that got their own cultural or private reasons. Me, I'm speaking economics"

"Brotha, white folks will bury you alive if you go down here thinking the South slow. The South ain't no happy hunting ground for niggas from up North no mo'. Shit done changed big time"

"But what about if a man had a new vision for the South? I see it as the capitol of the Thug Kingdom. I dream of a South with a strong economy fueled by thug money, see what I'm saying, son? In Miami, most of the hotels and big buildings were put up with dirty money although politicians try to scrub that fact out, but it's true. Damn near everything you see in Miami is standing because of narcotic money"

"And that's your vision, to re-build the South?"

Rah-Rah wiped his mouth with a silk napkin. "It's bigger than that, brer. I want to unify all the thugs under one set and then to strengthen the set. Don't laugh because I feel it"

"Niggas too destructive. What thug you know that ain't all for his goddamn self? But if you remember, you'll know that before this country was unified, they were thirteen colonies who did shit their own way. One day they woke up and realized that there was more power in unity"

"And you think you can do this with thugs, create a United Nation of Thugs?" Shine laughed. "Ain't happening, my man. I'm sorry"

"But can you blame a man from trying?"

"Naw, can't blame a playa for reaching for the stars"

"I dream of a Thug Kingdom where a thug can go as far as his heart and smarts will take him. I see a world where a thug; will enjoy financial opportunities he never thought possible"

"But why the South gotta be the headquarters?"

"Simple, son. The North dying, what crackers ain't picked cleaned, niggas have destroyed. The buzzards are circling up North while the South is vibrant, still untapped. Thugs can become a superpower down there, but we just need to be organized"

Suddenly, Rah-Rah's invasion of the South had not been pure madness after all. The nigga was ill with ambition and he desired the South as both a playground and a fortress, a honey hole where every thug would owe him props and allegiance.

"That's a heavy duty dream, Rah"

"But check out the rewards"

"Don't get me wrong, Rah-Rah, but you really are trying to imitate that white dude ---------what's his name?"

"Like I said, Warren Buffet my idol, but what I'm doing also is using some of the ideas of black economic empowerment as preached by Dr. Claud Anderson. I just thugged his concepts out. In his book PowerNomics, The National Plan to Empower Black America, I saw where I could put his idea to use and I intend to. He stressed out how we must organize and it's a blueprint for the Thug Kingdom I plan to establish. When I'm finished, the Thug Kingdom will be the first and only community strong enough to compete with the crackers almost dollar for dollar. The Thug Kingdom will be the beginning"

"Of what, Rah-Rah? Of what?"

"Of a Thug Heaven right here on earth, that's what"

"Why just thugs? What happens to all the other brothas who can't get into this heaven on earth? Why not let all black folk in?"

Rah-Rah spoke with both cleverness and calm. "I anticipated that question, son, and my answer is the same one a true believer in Jesus would give you if you asked him or her about why all people can't get into their Heavenly Kingdom: Some were meant to be left behind" Rah-Rah leaned closer, his voice turning edgier. "Why do you think it should be any different in the Thug Kingdom. Only those of us who have been true to the game can experience Thug rapture. No one else is deserving"

Fighting hard to keep his emotions in check, Shine suddenly realized how big a danger Rah-Rah was. The nigga saw his quest to smash the South as some kind of Holy War, but to hear him talk it was nothing.

Rah-Rah's voice grew cold. "The time is now, but silly niggas in the South will interfere with my plans"

"No offense, but you can't blame them. It's not like you wanting to go down there to trap off one of them phat-assed, juicy southern girls and make her your wife. You want to run the whole South. Damn, man, that's almost unbelievable. And what about them country thugs down there? Motherfuckas got gats too. You have thought about that, haven't you?"

Rah-Rah look disturbed. "Waiter!", he called out. "Check!"

On the stage at Magic City, the tall, long-legged dancer with the bee-stung lips had everybody's attention. Bandit was watching intently. The light-skinned girl before her had been fantastic, but the mixed breed bitch on the stage now was mesmerizing.

Bandit stared in spellbound amazement.

"Make it clap back!" Niggas stood around clapping their hands. "Make it clap back!", they screamed insanely. "Make that pussy clap!"

The girl seemed to be at peace on the stage, looking out into the vacant distance, but totally in control. She was caught up in the crunk and she was an expert at using the music to bring out all the freak in her. Like no other woman Bandit had ever seen dance, this bitch took advantage of the bass and knew how to make it bounce her beautiful ass up and down, round and round. From side to side.

When the sista fell down on all fours and then in one smooth motion doubled her body up until her phat ass was sticking up in the air like a church's steeple, and began to work it, niggas went stupid.

"Is that a goddamn crime or what?!" one brotha in an Armani suit yelled. "Do you know how many laws of gravity that bitch just broke. Goddamn, ain't she sweet?"

Late into the song, sista was back into biz'ness again, burning niggas eyes by flashing pure pussy. Now that the cheeks of her ass were glistening with sweat, the thong looked like it dug deeper between her thick thighs, and running her hands over her own body like it was an instrument, the dancer performed her own especially captivating version of the Hoola Hoop and just before the crunk had died down showed perfect execution of the 'fold over'. But niggas would have rioted if sista would have tried to exit the stage without doing the "Booty Clap" again. She turned the house inside out.

Bandit stuck a C-note in her garter belt as other niggas also compensated her well for that performance by tossing all denominations of bills at her red-painted toe-nails.

Bandit thought of scribbling the phone number of his hotel on another hundred dollar bill, but before he could, he felt a strong hand on his shoulder pulling him back. Turning, Bandit saw a tall, thin, old head standing there.

"You KoKo's man, Bandit?"

"Who you?"

"Thin Man"

"I've heard your name"

"So have a million more niggas. Let's have a drink. Bitches ain't going nowhere. They do, they'll come back. Hoes gotta pop their pussies. It's in their blood"

Bandit checked out the ole head. Nigga was sharp and none of that O.G. shit from back in the days either. Thin Man played a dark blue linen suit with a powder blue silk shirt, but what truly put the old head's gear on Go was the diamond studded 18-karat white and yellow gold cuff links that flashed fire at both his wrists.

"Old school?" Bandit pointed at the cuff links.

"My school, so don't try to rock my style when your young ass get back home"

Bandit laughed. "Okay, Thin Man, your flava safe. What you having. Drinks on me"

They ordered and made small talk while they waited.

"Be sure to tell your man that if it was anybody but him, I would tell him to talk to the undertaker, but the nigga my god-son and I don't want him out in no storm like the one I see coming. Anyway, his rear is covered from this end"

"He'll appreciate hearing that. Thanks"

Thin Man stood to leave. "By the way, that girl's name is Sasha"

"I'll remember that"

"Fuck that. Where you laying your head at, youngblood?"

Bandit told him.

"When you splitting back to Charlotte?"

Bandit told him.

"She'll holla at you before you go, playa"

Thin Man disappeared into the crowd.

Chapter 8

When Shine pulled up in front of Shark's Bar on 79th and Amsterdam, he thought of hollering out of the car's window at Rah-Rah until he saw that the brotha was not solo. What Shine noticed most about the pair with him was that they had the grim look of enforcers written all across their black faces.

Shine stayed in his whip for a while longer, studying the scene. Rah-Rah, who had on a dark brown Jack Victor suit and tan gators, talked and laughed while his two enforcers stood stiff as a marble statue.

Shine had come to meet Rah-Rah for lunch, but now something warned him to excuse himself because the two nigga goons made it clear that this lunch was not going to be polite. Shine realized that Rah-Rah was going to pop the big question today and he also recognized that if he gave the wrong answer or came up short in any way, he would vanish; come up missing.

As Shine got out of the 300C, the first thing Rah-Rah did was to step over to hug Shine and to examine the whip.

"Y'all dawgs down in VA be popping some serious tags" Rah-Rah nodded approvingly. "Whip fancy" Then his tone turned more serious. "Let's go in. Our table is waiting" Shine followed Rah-Rah to where the two brothas stood. "This Jaheim. This Flava. They gonna be dining with us this afternoon" He stared coldly at Shine. "You don't mind, do you?"

"Naw," Shine lied. "As long as they don't stick they hands in my plate 'cause I'm hungrier than a Hebrew slave"

"Well, dawg," Rah-Rah smiled. "Let's go fill up"

This afternoon everything about Rah-Rah appeared more purposeful as if he was determined to get something off his chest once and for all, even if it meant getting blood on his hands.

As the waiter took their orders, Shine realized how fast the situation was moving and he feared that if he didn't control his paranoia that shit could quickly spin out of control. Damn, he should have strapped up. What if Rah-Rah had found out who he actually was? Suppose Jalisa had flipped the script and had admitted to Rah-Rah that she had set him up? Such an admission would be more than a little embarrassing for him.

Though he was able to clock his fears for a brief second, the spasm in the pit of his stomach flared up once more when only two platters of food were returned to the table. One was set in front of him. The other was placed before Rah-Rah. The two goons didn't get shit, but they sat there like they were ready to retaliate if he didn't clean his plate, as if they would not tolerate a motherfucka wasting Rah-Rah's money.

After taking a few bites of his steak burger, Rah-Rah pushed the food away in annoyance. "It is vital that I get me a spot in VA" He didn't wait for a reaction. "And I want you to lead the way in" When Shine glanced up, Rah-Rah held his gaze. "To say no would prevent me from doing something that I have thought of doing for quite a long time"

"The Thug Kingdom thang?"

Rah-Rah nodded. "Along with some other issues that don't concern you right now"

"You already make it sound as though I have no choice"

"I had hoped you wouldn't have looked upon it as a choice because thugs have obligations to each other. Sometimes it is a thug's duty just to say yes" Rah-Rah's voice softened. "And when you fucking with a nigga like me, yes is never unreasonable. Know why? Because with a motherfucka like me, yes has its privileges"

Shine grinned. "What does no carry?"

Rah-Rah ignored the retort. "Where do niggas in VA cop from? DC and Philly?"

"The Richmond niggas do. Thugs on The Beach get our cookies from out of Florida"

"I know y'all ain't never spent with me. None of y'all, but fuck that. I'll throw you five keys for your services"

"Paper always makes such a nice bribe, I mean, gift"

Rah-Rah smiled widely. "I like your style, Shine, Ask for what you want, that's how you make shit happen. So what do you want? Dope or paper?"

"Both. "

Rah-Rah looked at Shine with slight amusement. "You a piece of work, but you can have it your way. Get my dawgs settled in and I'll show how generous I can be"

"No offense, Rah-Rah," Shine said cautiously, "but this ain't about your generosity or my salvation. What we have heah, in the simplest thug terms is two niggas doing each other a favor"

"And?"

"It means I want my shit up front"

"You got it"

"Good, now when do you want to hit VA?"

Old School slow jams softly whispered out of the speakers of the CD player while the turned down lights, dimmed to a slow-burning sensual glow casting satiny shadows upon the bed where Shine and Janeen laid.

The Chateau Piada Sauternes had gone to Janeen's head in such a delightful way, the sweet fragrance of fruit and walnuts dancing on her tongue as she kissed Shine deeply. She left sexually inspired. All her inner inhibitions had been tossed to the wind long ago, opening the door for the release of her youthful freaks.

She trembled with pleasure and desire as she experienced the fire of Shine's fingers upon her delicate, chocolate skin, caressing the flesh where her blouse and bra used to be.

Neither had spoken for quite sometime, the mood more important than speech, but when Shine moved his hands lower, sighs and moans escaped Janeen's lips, filling the room with the strong message of just how turned ON she was. At no other time had she ever wanted to fuck this badly. She needed to get her pussy slaughtered, to have dick disappearing in and out of her womb to the intoxicating sounds of Smokey Robinson's wonderful falsetto.

Via touch, Janeen got her first nut! It rumbled through every fiber of her being and shook her pussy walls with so much force that it felt like her clitoris had been beheaded!

"What happened?" Shine teased.

"My kitty kat exploded"

90

"Want me to do it again?"

Janeen nodded. "But if you keep on, my kitten gonna turned into a tiger"

Shine softly grabbed Janeen's hands and put it on his dick. "What you have there is a tiger tamer"

Janeen rubbed Shine's dick. "Oh my God!" she squealed. "I didn't know they came in this size!"

Sucking her neck like it was a succulent grape, Shine began to trail long wet kisses all over her shoulders and onto her swollen breasts. Using his tongue, Shine teased first one titty, then the other. Janeen gripped Shine's ears as if they were chocolate handlebars, holding on as her body shuddered with electricity. She felt the fire.

"No disrespect, Janeen, but you will no longer be a child when I turn you loose"

"Then, make me a woman," Janeen begged. "Fill me up with your manhood"

And at that moment Shine made Janeen's eyes light up as he excited her rock hard nipples by gnawing gently on them with his teeth. Janeen, in response, cupped her breast, feeding Shine more dark flesh.

Janeen had never been in the company of such an expert tongue and she found herself smiling as she dreamed what joy it would bring when it found its way inside her pussy.

As Shine moved closer to her secret garden, Janeen's pussy had already begun to exude its intoxicating scent, addressing the bedroom with the musky fragrance of sexual delirium.

"Taste my nectar, baby," she pleaded. "Eat my fruit"

Shine affectionately greeted Janeen's moist pussy lips with the tip of his tongue, slicing through the wet opening, parting the hair until he discovered the black pearl he sought. Janeen, Shine learned, owned a delicately constructed clit that protruded from her vagina like a stem of black silk. He dined

91

on it, nibbling on the delectable morsel of skin, noticing that when he caught the plump fold of flesh between his teeth and gently grinded against it in a see-sawing motion that Janeen's ass bounced up and down off the bed in tune with the sex-induced music of her own moans.

A stranger to this type of pussy-sucking, Janeen's beautiful face screwed up into a mask of pleasure and after uttering a long litany of obscene curses, she thanked Shine for making her feel like a glorified slut.

Janeen then experienced a second orgasm. This time her cum felt thick like a cream sauce, but Shine drank pussy juice from the goblet of her velvety vagina until she was both sedated and empty.

Her speech slurred, her eyes shut, and her breathing slowed, Janeen gently pushed Shine's head away. "Stop!", she screamed. "I can't take any more. I feel too good"

Shine rolled over, laying alongside her, his lips glowing with her liquid flava, he tickled her playfully. "I call that cowardice"

"My pussy feel so good it's almost like you done opened it up and worked some magic on it"

Shine rolled on top of Janeen. "And that was only my introduction" Shine played with the swollen lips of her pussy, getting Janeen ready, arousing her.

Within seconds, Janeen was sex-drunk again and unprovoked she stretched her pussy lips open even further "Ride me like a horse, Shine" She caressed his dick, touching it against the slit of her pussy. "Fuck me, baby. Wet me with your cum"

Sweating, Shine pushed his dick through the slit, feeling her puffy pussy lips part softly, folding up on either side of his dick like high-priced butter. Still only halfway in, Shine felt Janeen's body tremble and shake as another orgasmic earthquake simmered deep down inside her, setting itself OFF in tiny electric waves that burst open around his dick.

Careful not to rush, Shine remained frozen in mid-air with only half of his dick inside Janeen until he sensed she was ready for more. Easing himself in slowly, he tried to shake the thought that he might be hurting her, but when he saw the glazed expression of lust etched on her lovely face, he slipped the remainder of hard dick into her.

Janeen moaned, thrust her hips up and down a few times then wrapped her arms around his neck. "Dick me down, baby. I'm ready"

Fully mounted in the saddle, Shine set the pace, a slow tempo rhythm that allowed him to massage the walls of Janeen's pussy thoroughly, but as her juices lubricated his dick and wet her insides more he picked up the pace, shifting into a faster mode. Janeen instinctively switched into gear with him, rotating her phat ass much more quickly while her clit stood at attention.

Wanting to deliver as much thrust and friction as possible, Janeen wrapped her legs around Shine's waist, stacking his long dick up more firmly against her stomach. She was full.

Fucking now with wild abandon, Shine and Janeen increased the pace again, going back and forth, round and round, up and down. And when they could inflict no more pleasure upon one another, they nutted in unison.

Ten toes up and ten toes down.

Janeen and Shine could offer each other nothing more, except tender kisses, and after basking in the afterglow of their fucking they both fell asleep.

KoKo went to bed later than usual. He was not 100% at peace with what he had to do or the short amount of time in which he had to accomplish it, but 72 hours was all he was given. After that, the window of opportunity would close forever.

Seeing that he wasn't going to get any sleep, KoKo almost decided to phone Kendra, but just as suddenly, dropped the idea. Both she and Janeen would fly in tomorrow. KoKo beamed. That was the good part. Three days later, Shine would leave New York for Virginia Beach. That was the bad news.

When Shine arrived in Virginia Beach (his true hometown) with Rah-Rah's peeps, shit had to be in place to make Shine appear to be a major figure in the city. When the nigga touched down, he had to get mad props because if this episode of the plan failed, the whole game would be lost.

KoKo had already worked a miracle by transforming a dropshot into a bonafide playa, yet now he had to groom all the bit actors to play their roles, but instead of being absolutely discouraged KoKo viewed himself as a director on the set of his newest movie. He merely had to stage his props and to get all the other actors into character and all would be well just like in Hollywood. At least that what he hoped.

As the concepts began to take form in his head, KoKo slipped a Trillville CD in the player and amped up crunk blasted the bedroom. Neva Eva was capable of bringing the noize.

Rumor had it that there was a lot more to Virginia Beach than the come-up tales of Missy Elliott, Timberland, Magoo, and The Neptunes. There were also thug niggas from out of Lake Edward, Bayside Arms, and Plaza who were clocking paper and moving product 24/7. Plus, you had niggas from Norfolk who came over and worked the block also.

The inescapable conclusion was that KoKo was going to have to borrow one of these crews and use them as his cheering section for Shine. KoKo imagined that it wouldn't be easy and that he wouldn't stand a ghost of a chance of pulling off unless he clued the niggas in on what was truly going down. And that was where the greatest danger was. Being that he was totally in the blind about who was loyal to whom, he could put himself in a very ugly position since it just might be that one of the VA crews had mad love for the niggas up top. It was no damn secret that practically all the yayo that flooded the hood in Virginia Beach came from out of New York, so it stood to reason that there might be more to the bond than a buyer/seller relationship. And that could fuck shit up bigtime.

KoKo understood how dope buyers would do damn near anything to collect brownie points with their sellers in the hope of securing better prices and KoKo doubted that a greedy nigga would sit on this type info without trying to cash in. But who could blame him? Nigga would get mad love (and discounts) from New York if he exposed the Southern boys' game plan.

That VA had to be the spot from which he had to trap the New York niggas off did not seem right with KoKo since VA was so close to up top, the State was almost like the suburbs to the North, and a lot of hustlers from DC treated VA like it was one great, big goddamn mall where they could go down and take what the fuck they wanted and then zoom on back across the border to the District. But that just might be the meal ticket KoKo was-looking for. Maybe the VA thugs were tired of being looked upon as the outskirts of the North and tired of niggas from up top raiding their hood for paper and pussy.

KoKo was sorry that he didn't have a more solid plan and though his agenda was by no means trump tight, he had to roll with it. He had already reasoned that he couldn't buy these niggas' allegiance so he wouldn't deny them the truth. He would give up the whole spill about the upcoming Thug War and hoped they got the picture because of all the turf in

95

the Bottom they were the most vulnerable due to their close proximity to the enemy. No doubt, VA would be hit first since the armies of the North could practically strike out at them from their own backyards.

KoKo would simply be straight up and point out the danger. He would point out also how sad he was that it had come to this and he would be sure to stress that he understood that VA had not asked for this war, but neither had Charlotte, Atlanta, Memphis, or the rest of the South. Yet the clock was ticking and they had no choice but to kill or be killed and now that first blood had already been drawn, it was far too late to kiss and make up.

It was do or die.

On Saturday morning, KoKo sent out three carloads of his Westside Connection up the highway to Interstate 264. Their mission was to pow-wow with all the major figures in Virginia Beach, Hampton Roads, and The Tidewater area, to bring the brothas the news, and to let them know that there was no other way to deal with the Northern menace. VA would have to know that the threat was real and that though there was work to be done elsewhere, VA had to assume the role of guardian for the whole South.

What else could KoKo do? Not a damn thing.

The Casablanca on Princess Annie Road was a thug sanctuary and all the ballers in the Tidewater area of VA wouldn't risk not being spotted at the club on the regular, but this was Bandit's first time in the joint and a thousand thoughts raced through his head as he made his way to the small bar.

Local thugs gave Bandit and his two bodyguards the eye, but none of them made any funny moves or made any disrespectful gestures towards the three out-of-town niggas, and Bandit interpreted that as a sign of Big Gip's influence and power in the area. Word had already gone out via word-of-mouth that Gip was expecting a trio of strangers to show up at the Casablanca and since they were his guest, they weren't to be made to feel uncomfortable. In addition, club management was to treat them to an open tab on the house.

At the bar, Bandit and his team were quickly served drinks while the bartender whispered that Gip would be in later and for them to enjoy themselves until his arrival. After the drinks, as if on cue, three scantily clad sistas who fit the profile of being dime-pieces boldly introduced themselves.

The sistas who were actual sisters provided wonderful entertainment for the Charlotte niggas, but just as soon as the conversation turned to late night bedroom activity, Gip showed up and the bitches vanished like smoke from a cigarette.

"Follow me," Gip commanded in a raspy voice, "let's step in the back"

In the back was a pool room where a bunch of niggas were either shooting pool or rolling dice. Either way a lot of money was changing hands and no one showed any interest in the three niggas from Carolina. Even Gip appeared to be in a hurry to get rid of them, but evidently he had gotten the word that this wasn't no standard thug bullshit these niggas were kicking so he was okay with investing an hour or so to get an earful of street gospel.

Gip raised his arm over his head like he was in church testifying to The Lord and out of a corner emerged a bitch who looked like Christina Milian only with more titties and ass. When Gip whispered in her ear his voice took on a more muted quality that suggested he had known the ho in a biblical sense. The fine, phat girl strolled off, but shortly returning with a tray of drinks as if running errands for Gip was as normal for her as slanging pussy.

"Grey Goose, gentlemen" Gip chimed, "the best vodka on the face of the earth" He raised his glass. "Here's to happy endings"

Bandit, a brown-skinned brotha with a short man's complex, whose main approach to life was to jump right in and to start throwing punches, patiently made small talk while the drinks were being consumed. According to thug etiquette, when you were on another man's turf it was improper to bring up biz'ness matters until the host opened the door for the conversation.

The Christina Milian girl popped up again, but this time it was more to get looked at than anything else. Bitch was spectacular, but Gip dismissed her.

"So you guys have a problem?"

Bandit was slightly distressed by the chill in Gip's voice, the way the nigga said it made it sound like Charlotte was in the wrong. "It's more like <u>we</u> have a problem. It's being considered a Southern problem and my man KoKo hoping we, the whole South, can line up together and close ranks on the threat"

Gip laughed. "So now Charlotte calling shots for the Bottom. First, it was Atlanta until them niggas' head swole up so big they believe they in a world all to themselves. And now it's Charlotte" Gip was an older cat, pushing 40 but still had position in VA. "It's kinda hard for me to remember when I first heard it or who said it, but the word was out a long time ago that one day niggas from Charlotte was gonna make a move to be the leaders of the New South. And damn, that shit was word. Charlotte now the number two financial center in the country, got the NFL and the crackers in the NBA bent over like bitches to put another basketball franchise down there once the Hornets split-----"

"Brotha, this ain't about white bread Charlotte. This about how the other half lives, the thug community. But it's even deeper than just me and the boys in the hood. The threat is against all of us from VA down to the ATL" Bandit stared Gip down. "So let's not get thangs out of context"

"Chill out, youngblood," Gip responded blankly. "I ain't never pretended to have no love from the cats up North and Lord knows I've had my share of run-ins with them over the years, but I don't need this. A goddamn war. How the fuck anybody gonna get any money if everybody's shooting at everybody else and his brother?"

"So that's your reason, money?"

There was a brief silence that both men needed to use to cool their tempers. It didn't do any good.

"You don't need to know my reasons, youngblood. All you need to know is that VA don't want no Dodge City shit in our zip code. While the rest of you deep South niggas down in the bottom running in and out of bitches, and gripping the grain on your tricked out whips, motherfuckas up heah making deals with the devil to keep the up North thugs out of our shit. VA the first spot on the Southern map so when niggas from up North and DC want to get some southern pussy or to test southern fire power, where you think they show up at. Right on our doorsteps, but have you ever heard us bitch to the rest of y'all niggas down below? Hell no. We fought our own private wars and a lot of brave soldiers gave up the ghost so that VA could do its own thang------"

"But this time it's different," Bandit yelled.

Pounding on the table, Gip yelled back. "No, the fuck it ain't either"

Silence.

"Look, homeys," Gip remarked calmly. "It's late and I know y'all been on the road so I'll tell you what. I'm gonna give you twenty minutes to convince me that fighting a war is better than getting paper"

"Man, you gonna miss it if you go at it like that," Bandit pleaded. "That's like trying to convince a motherfucka in jail that jacking his dick better than getting real pussy"

Gip broke out laughing. "Damn, nigga, whoooeee, you put that out there" He slapped the edge of the table playfully. "I like the fuck out of that, gonna use it too, first chance I get"

"It's yours. Feel free to drop it whenever you want to"

"Anyway, run your drama past me and I'll see what I think. Then tomorrow I'll go into council with Lil' Ted and Black Mike. We'll vote and then I'll holla at you cats 'round three"

The Christina Milian look-alike appeared with another tray of drinks and a blunt.

Shine rolled over, a sly grin on his face. "That's just your lil' ol' pussy talking. You don't love me"

"I do too"

"We just starting fucking yesterday and now you already in love. I mean, don't get me wrong, Janeen, you could be the one 'cause you got it all. You a 4 B bitch. You got Brains, Beauty, Boobs and Booty. But right now you also got innocence"

"And what's wrong with innocence?"

"It's allows you to fall head-over-heels in love with the first nigga who put dick to you right. That other nigga you was giving the pussy to wasn't nuthin' but a child himself. Young motherfucka was experimenting, didn't know shit about how to please a woman. Motherfucka so wet behind the ears that he probably think eating pussy a sin or something"

"I know what I feel"

"And?"

"I wanna be your woman. I'm a good bitch, Shine. All I need is a chance to prove myself. That's all I ask"

Shine stood up and walked over to the window, quietly watching the rain beat against the window pane. He was enchanted with Janeen. She was the most stunningly beautiful woman he had ever been with and though he was ten years older than she was, it didn't matter to him. The sista was passionate in bed and though he wasn't about to confess it right now, her youthful innocence was a priceless joy. He could very easily imagine how far ahead she'd be of the rest of the woman in NC once she gained more life experience.

He could already sense Janeen's devotion, knowing that her dedication to a real man would be as fine-tuned and as strong as her big sista's. It would bring him immense pleasure to watch Janeen grow into a woman. That would probably be the most rewarding experience of his life.

Shine recalled how sexually curious Janeen was, how she was willing to explore any bedroom activity to satisfy her man. He thought back with unrestrained delight on how she had bathed him once they had finished fucking, how she had oiled his head and given him a pedicure. The girl was all that.

The rain picked up, splattering even harder against the glass pane.

"Janeen," Shine said softly, "go put on something pretty. Hurry up"

Janeen excitedly dressed up in some fly sportwear from Dollhouse. She had quickly fixed her hair. "How you like this outfit, daddy?"

"It's lovely"

"Now, what?"

"Go stand out in the rain!"

Without a word, Janeen went outside.

Chapter 9

Justice was butt naked under the towel and the Asian girl was gently massaging his shoulder, kneading the kinks out of his rock hard muscles. He closed his eyes, the weed still buzzing in his head, and almost forget he had Rah-Rah on the other end of the phone.

"Yeah, yeah, no problem. It was a touchdown............No doubt ....Nigga Shine a minor legend down here so we got the red carpet treatment...........We in and this spot is sweeter than church ....Yeah, yeah, I'll call you tomorrow. Out"

Rah-Rah looked at the phone as if he had just hit the jack-pot. Every time he tried to suppress his emotions they popped up like the animated color graphics on the video game he had been playing.

To clear his mind he tried to get back into Manhunt on his Play-station 2, but by now his adrenaline for the graphic action had faded and he found he couldn't sustain his interest. Other shit was on his mind.

He switched OFF the machine.

At last, he was in! And if things went off according to plan Rah-Rah now held the destiny in hand. And it gave him great satisfaction to know that a New World Order for thugs was no longer an impossible dream. Stomping in VA was the first step and he saw no reason why or how he should or could fail. This should be a GO.

Rah-Rah recalled being on Riker's Island after he had gotten caught up in a gun battle with a Puerto Rican gang over turf and he had realized then that life was much too important to lose over a few slabs of concrete pavement. He remembered his own frustration at watching niggas come in the joint for long bids for shit that wasn't worth it, and he saw that the madness would continue as long as the street were not under the lock of a single ruler who could establish a uniform Thug Code for niggas all across the country.

Although Rah-Rah didn't enjoy trying on the personalities of men who had come before him, he did --------- in a distant kind of way---------view himself as Moses, The Lawgiver and over and over again, he told himself that thugs needed him. They needed him to lay down the law. They needed him to stop the senseless, shameless violence. They needed him to rule over them.

With very few exceptions, packed prisons proved that thugs would have no hope without the iron fist of a strong leader. This would be The Renaissance where niggas would hustle with finesse, thereby eliminating the need for and the requirements of mayhem.

Soon they would know. Soon he would unite the thugs of the nation. Soon he would declare himself king.

Justice decided he didn't want shit to do with these country boys----------or girls but he wouldn't stop the rest of his posse from interacting with the regulars. If the New Yorkers wanted to hang out and fuck these Southern bitches that was fine with him. He planned to maintain a polite distance but he had to admit that Virginia Beach did possess a certain charm, so charming in fact that the English had chosen a nearby spot, which they named Jamestown, to drop off the first load of slaves to ever touch down in this country. What kind of rep was that for your set?

But that didn't concern Justice. He hated the South, feeling that nothing about it agreed with him. The hot-assed weather annoyed him, the green grass made him sick, and the slow niggas and silly hoes were enough to drive him mad. If he had his way he would destroy everything below the Mason-Dixie Line.

"Here let me hit that again for you, homey"

The man's voice brought Justice back to the here and now and he stuck out his white styrofoam cup. The man refilled it with Hennessey.

"Don't get to see many people from the neighborhood around these parts, so it's a treat when Harlem comes to town" C.B., a transplanted New Yorker, owned and operated a boutique across the street from Booker T. Washington High School. He had been in Virginia Beach for over a decade.

"How you stand it down here?" Justice asked.

C.B. grinned. "Had to leave Harlem. The block was hot so I got in the wind. Went far enough South to get out of the line of fire of niggas who were hunting for me, but not far enough to get countrified, see what I'm saying?" C.B. who had gotten fat over the years still was light on his feet because when the phone rang, the brotha floated and shuffled off as smoothly as Muhummad Ali in his prime.

While C.B. was on the horn, Justice kept thinking that he should try to pry some info out of the brotha about these country niggas' attitude. Justice believed in the old adage that in order to defeat an enemy, you first had to know him. He also had the gut instinct that C.B. Could be a big help to his mission, but he couldn't risk revealing anything of the real reason he was in VA.

C.B. was laughing when he came back to the front of the store. "My wife bought my alibi about where I was last night. That was her calling to apologize for going off on my ass this morning"

"And that's what was so funny?", Justice asked.

"Hell yeah. That call just saved me about a grand. I was going out at lunch and buy the ol' girl a piece of jewelry, you know, a peace offering. Now, I ain't buying her shit" C.B. laughed some more. "The thing to remember when you start stepping out on your ol' lady is to make sure that all the cutie-pies who are going to be the usual suspects in your girl's mind know how to lie"

"Thanks for the advice"

"The least I can do for a Harlemite"

"Tell me about these cats down here. Do they got heart or are they soft?"

C.B. shook his head. "Ain't no nigga nowhere in America soft. Nigga can't afford to be weak, but there is a difference in the way niggas carry it from hood to hood. You got to understand that the strive is a lot harder in Harlem or out in Watts than it would ever be in Seven Cities"

"Seven Cities?"

"Mainly a reference to the 7 cities in Virginia that make up the complete Tidewater area. Local spots carry drama, just not on the scale or with the depth as a 'for-real' stomp down ghetto. Everything here mostly about the beach or the military"

"But niggas get paper?"

"All the time"

"Hmmph", Justice snorted. "I ain't never heard of a hood where a nigga can clock paper without mad drama"

"A lot of things are possible once you leave New York. Being out of Harlem gave me a whole new way of looking at things"

"I guess you right. Ain't no place in the world like Harlem. At least the old Harlem" Justice sipped from his cup. He guessed it was time to find out a little something about his most gracious host. "So, tell me, what kind of bailer is Shine?"

"Who?"

"Shine" Justice laughed. "Don't tell me you don't know who Shine is? Shit, homeboy. Everybody knows Shine"

"I don't and I know all the major bailers in town. All of 'em spend with me. You got T-Money_____"

"Fuck T-Money for a second. You don't know Shine. Is that what you telling me?"

"Naw, homey, ain't'no nigga named Shine doing nothing big in this spot unless he on the down low and you know what they say when a nigga too low down on the down low"

"Put me down to what they be saying. I'm green to this Southern slang"

"When a nigga clocking that big and ain't nobody can see where his money coming from, brotha might be working for the feds, see what I'm saying?"

For a second, Justice was speechless. "Brer, listen, I'm speaking of money-getting Shine who got a mansion on the South side of the Beach…"

"That's where he lives?"

"Yeah, and I have been inside the crib. Phat to death"

"What it look like?"

"Shit, what a mansion supposed to look like? This crib cream, lots of window, palm trees and shit out front, grey-looking roof. Bitch big"

C.B. scratched his jaw. "Man, that's Timbaland's crib. I'm telling you, ain't no nigga named Shine live up there. You better check dude out. I ain't trying to get in your business but you just might have Smokey The Bear on your tail" C.B. set his cup down. "Now we homeys and all, but if you got heat on you I can't stand the feds looking into my shit. Plus, I ain't wanting to end up on the wrong end of a drug or murder conspiracy. I hope that kind of misery ain't tailing you, but kinda keep your distance if you hot, see what I'm saying"

"It's cool old-timer and it's like I told you earlier, I'm just passing through"

"Don't matter to me, playa, but if I were you------ "

"Say no more. Glad to meet you"

At the D.J. Booth Justice was told that it would be about 30 minutes before he could get his request put on the turntable.

Justice slipped the DJ a CD and a fifty dollar bill and went back to his table.

Other than wanting the hear his song there wasn't much else about the club that interested him. And even though Harlem Nights was up to the roof with phat hoes

Justice didn't have his radar out, so the most he would serve the bitches with was an expressionless glare. When a ghetto fabulous dame sashayed up and pretended she was in need of male companionship Justice mumbled something about he was a Baptist minister who was simply out to get a good look at sinful women so he would have some "breaking news" type shit for his Sunday sermon.

As the bitch huffed off, Justice upside down at the empty spots at his tables. He hoped this would get the message out that he wanted to be left completely alone but if the upside down glasses didn't discourage motherfuckas then he would pimp smack the next female who stepped into his private zone.

It was several minutes later that a high yellow ho was on the verge of making the mistake of crossing the invisible line when she noticed the *cold* glare in Justice's face, quickly deciding that there were things a lot worse than missing a play to score a free drink. She turned and patted her ass at Justice before bouncing off.

When the sound system boomed out. "Who Gives A Fuck Where You From" by Three 6 Mafia, Justice nodded his head to give quiet props to his homey DJ Kay Slay because the beats had come off his Street Sweeper Vol 2. CD.

The Lyrics and the industrial strength bass had the whole club on its feet. The dance floor was ass-to-ass packed as niggas and bitches competed ferociously for any empty space that was available so they could stick body parts in it. An arm here, a leg there, a phat ass going round and round. All motherfuckas wanted was room enough to maneuver enough to embarrass the dancers next to them.

Shit was off the chain!

Justice observed in wonder as he saw one bitch in a yellow pantsuit orbiting about two niggas like she was the sun. Another nigga, probably a soldier on leave or AWOL, was standing in place, pumping his knees up and down like his black ass was marching. To the left, a big bitch who should have been charged a double admission fee was broke down over some skinny motherfucka's thigh like a shotgun and he had hiked her blue spandex dress up over her HUGE butt and was working her mountainous cheeks like she was possessed. Big bitch had on a pair of reflective draws.

Then everything crashed. The dancers looked around in panic for only a second before they started howling and screaming like the DJ had, all of a sudden, betrayed them, as if he had stabbed them in the back musically.

"TAKE THAT SHIT OFF!!" The crowd shouted. "STICK THAT SONG UP YOUR WIFE"S ASS!"

With a hot nanosecond the DJ yanked the Lil' Scrappy CD he had gotten from Justice off the turntable and quickly replaced it with some Missy Elliott. A wild roar went up from the crowd and just like that asses were rocking again. The DJ realizing how the mistake he had made could have gotten him a serious beatdown, then whipped the sweat from his brow and then sent to the bar for a double shot of Courvoisier to celebrate his narrow escape.

Justice gave the DJ a minute to calm his nerves before he trekked to the DJ booth. The DJ looked like he wanted to spit on Justice.

"No more goddamn requests," the DJ yelped. "You see that shit"

"What the fuck happened? I don't get it"

"Niggas in VA ain't with that Crunk shit. If I would've been on the -b and paying attention I wouldn't have let that bullshit touch my turntable"

"But Crunk the big shit in the South"

"Not in VA"

"This still the South, ain't it?"

"Where you from, dawg?"

"New York"

CRUNK

"That's why you don't know then"

"I know that the South biting on this Crunk and I know Virginia down home"

"We down home, but we ain't South like that"

Justice acted as tough he was confused. "That ain't what a nigga learn in geography class. The map in the books say VA south. Now, y'all might not like it, but that's what the white man say"

"Hold up" The DJ freaked his turntable, using a technique that drove the club-goers into a frenzy. The beat was so amped and hyped that bitches started throwing panties at the DJ booth to show love.

"Damn", Justice was impressed.

"I just perfected that technique"

"Motherfucka on cue, no doubt about that" Justice shrugged. "Maybe you need to bottle that up and sell it"

The DJ laughed. "But back to what I was saying. We South by geography, but we North by attitude. That's why we don't fuck with CRUNK. As far as I'm concerned they need to keep that noise in the deep bottom. Up here, we take our cue from your homeboys in New York. Before we got our own spotlight from people like Missy and Magoo, rappers down here were trying to copy Wu-Tang. Ain't nobody up here never rode Lil' Jon or Luda's jock"

"I just thought-----------"

"And that's another thing. If you ever want to find out how deep down a nigga's root go in the bottom, this is a failproof test. The more he like Crunk, the deeper he from in the South. And as you can see, we hate that shit"

"So what that mean"

"We North"

"But say the Civil War broke out again, which side would VA be on?"

111

"Shit, dawg, we rolling with y'all"

Justice smiled. Rah-Rah would be glad to hear that. Justice checked his watch. It was too early in the a.m. to call New York, so he wouldn't fuck with Rah to let him know just how correctly his little experiment had played itself out. It was Rah-Rah who had decided that the Crunk tape would be a good way to feel out which way the wind blew in VA and if tonight was any indication, nigga in this town really didn't have much in common with the niggas farther down the line. That was A-plus news because if VA wanted to rock the up North flava they would have to side with the niggas from New York when the shit hit the fan.

Tonight was just a test, but VA had passed with flying colors. At close to two in the morning, Justice left Harlem Nights and he was feeling so good when he jumped into his Saab, he jammed Missy Elliott's new CD *This Is Not A Test* into the car's stereo system. Justice loved the title. Sista must have ESP, know shit about ready to get out of control.

But speaking of tests, Justice figured it was about time Shine got put to one. Motherfucking nigga better study hard because death was not a passing grade.

This is not a test!

Chapter 10

Justice didn't want Shine to think he was bugging so he made sure he kept his feelings secret and dealt mainly with the brotha only when it was necessary. The free minutes gave him some extra time to spy on the nigga but even when he was shopping for information, Justice was as discreet as possible. Rah-Rah had schooled him well in the science of manipulating motherfuckas.

So far, Justice had studied a wide range of shit that made Shine suspect. True, if this was a police by KoKo, Shine was playing the game well, yet the nigger had missed things. Overlooking or ignoring shit could reflect disaster. But then again, Justice had to give-ups to plain ol' good luck because that is what it was that had taken him out to C.B.'s boutique. Nothing more than the desire to touch bases with an old head from Harlem, but it was that auspicious meeting that had him dying to find out if Shine was breathing fire on them. The stuff he had uncovered at this point hadn't done much to soften his distrust of Shine, but it still wasn't quite enough to torture the nigga over. Yet, Justice did wonder how the nigga would explain being up in Timbaland's crib? Simple. As a dope boy, he couldn't get the crib in his own scribe so he used Timbaland, who was both squeaky clean and legit, to handle the name game. Justice could hear Shine now, but what might not be so easy to explain was the whip. Came to find out the motherfucka had been bought in, of all places, Charlotte! Now, that was interesting. For the time being Justice was in the process of finding out who the people were that owned the KC Complex. They were the same people who'd purchased the ride, paying hard cash for it.

"Explain that, nigga", Justice said to himself, but in his mind he could already see himself questioning Shine with the 9 to the busta's head. Inside him he experienced an urgent need to sort this situation out quickly because irregardless of if it was a sting or an ambush, time was running out.

He resisted the urge to notify Rah-Rah. This was about the third or fourth time he had gotten that idea, but he was determined to dig a little deeper first.

The next morning after eating breakfast, Justice hit the shower, got fresh in his Sean John gear and was about to head out when he got the return phone call he had been expecting.

After the brief exchange of info Justice expressed his appreciation by kicking out a big cash bonus to his peeps on the other end of the line. He hung up, feeling vindicated. He had not been mistaken. Shine was a goddamn phony. Fuck how clever the ploy had been because the gig was over. The nigga was busted and fixing to get wrecked.

Now, it was time to phone New York. Rah-Rah would want to hear this shit although he wouldn't believe it. The K C

Complex in Charlotte was owned by Kenny Combs, who just happened to be KoKo, the same nigga they had major beef with.

Some blood had to flow, without delay.

Soon!

Bandit wasn't impressed by the New York niggas. He felt the adrenaline snap, crackle, and pop in his body as he waited on the right moment to finish his mission. He would give the niggas another 48 hours to live and then he would move on them, destroying every last one of the bastards. He wondered why KoKo wanted to wait so long, but perhaps there was a good enough explanation for it. They really didn't need the extra time. Plus they had the niggas lined up like ducks in a shooting gallery, but KoKo had insisted they wait to see if any more of the up North crew was going to roll in as a support column. As far as he could tell, though, this was it. Justice, the leader, had given no indication that Rah-Rah was sending down more troopers, but like KoKo had commented, just because the news was not communicated didn't mean it wasn't going to go down. KoKo had also repeatedly informed him that war was not the occasion for wild speculation. The point was well taken.

Still, Bandit could feel the pressure. Shit could collapse at any given moment and Bandit didn't want anything to happen that could void the edge Charlotte now possessed and that could very well occur if these niggas weren't taken to the killing floor real soon. Virginia Beach was a pressure cooker with the two crews working together and Bandit knew that the least little incident could blow the scenario up. Already the New Yorkers had brought attitude with them, acting as if they were the Masters of the Universe while the Westside

115

Connection from Charlotte had to play along with the game until they were given the okay to strike.

The shit was boiling and even though they had only been in town a few days the New Yorkers had already been bold enough to suggest that nothing go down on the block without their permission. They flaunted their assumed superiority and made it clear that they had to build a new way of doing biz'ness from scratch because the country way of getting paid was too wack and too slow. Bandit didn't know how much longer he could hold the fort down if New York kept the bullshit up. The Westside Connection had already bent over backwards to accommodate these niggas and Bandit was tired of seeing his boys getting dissed, so he made up his mind.

One more day.

The next morning Justice surprised Bandit with a house call. He appeared hyped to death, blunted. "Round up all your mob and jet over to Shine about ten"

"What up?"

"Some dawgs of mine in the industry want to do a video shoot with all of us in it", Justice spoke excitedly. "Nigga, we going to be in a video and guess who else flying down this morning for the video?"

"Who?"

"Does the name Jessica Rabbit ring a bell---------"

"You-you mean Mellysa Ford?"

"Yes sir, son, she on with us. Also that Puerto Rican sista from Jersey with the phat-to-death ass. And then my dawg say they sending down Eboni Jackson, the girl in Chingy's 'Right Thurr"

CRUNK

Justice was in gear, all G-Unit shit. He didn't ask to come in so both men stood on the front porch, the early morning breeze blowing in the smells of bacon frying on somebody's stove.

A police car rolled by. Both men ignored it.

"I'11 walk you out to your ride," Bandit offered.

"I'm cool, son. What you need to do is to start getting up with your people so we can get this video rolling. We probably gonna debut on 106th and Park so tell everyone to put on some extra floss. The director says he wants all of us to represent"

"Whose video is it?"

Justice patted Bandit on the shoulder playfully. "You'll find out when you get there. See ya"

Bandit watched Justice stroll to his car and though he tried not to read too much into the video announcement, the news, for some reason, made his blood turn cold. He stood on his porch even after Justice had driven down the block, abruptly turning left, disappearing from sight. Bandit thought about Jessica Rabbit, trying to let his anxiety slide, but there were too many threads to ignore.

Bandit was so nervous he decided to phone KoKo, but as soon as he got back inside the crib, his own horn was blowing.

"Yo," he muttered cautiously.

"Oh, man, shit, I forgot to tell you something else" Justice's voice still had amp but now it sounded more contrived, like the nigga was fronting. "You getting ready to hit up your peep?"

"Yeah. What up?"

"Tell them niggas not to bring no straps. That's what I forgot to mention. It'll get the director and the production crew all nervous, see what I'm saying" Justice made a chucking noise. "As quiet as it's kept, I think half the

117

motherfuckas that be working the shoot on probation or parole so they can't be around no jimmies. So handle that with your peeps and I'll get up with you at the spot. One"

Now Bandit was on red alert. This video situation was sounding more and more like a train wreck by the minute and a feeling of dread settled over him like a black shroud. He couldn't remember the last time he had asked his boys to journey naked. A thug never left his weapon at home and he was not going to demand that of the Westside Connection. Niggas were going to ride hard and that was that. Once they got to shine's crib and he spoke with the director personally, then he might give the order for his crew to leave their guns inside their vehicles, but not until then. If Justice didn't like that, then they could handle it personally. He wasn't sure whether Justice knew anything with his hands or not, but Bandit wouldn't be afraid to step out with him. Big muscles didn't mean a motherfucking thang, especially when you couldn't hit what you couldn't see.

Bandit laughed. *Punk-ass nigga better not roll like that unless an ass-whooping was something the nigga wasn't afraid of wearing.* Then reality set in. Hand-to-hand combat was too old school, was not the way 21st century thugs handled a grudge or settled a beef. Fist fighting had no relevance now that the laws of the streets had evolved into a more souped-up vision of retribution. Payback was a motherfucka. That was Chapter One of the new version of *The Thug Get-Down Manual*.

Bandit made the phone calls.

Looking up at the nerdy-looking dude, Bandit felt a bit more relaxed.

"Yeah, my man, we flew in from the West Coast last night and we hope to wrap this shoot up quickly because I'm on a tight shoot schedule" The director looked over his shoulder angrily. "Aggie, please don't tell me that you still haven't heard anything about when we can expect our video vixen!"

"No sir," Mr. Jeter, I'll try the airlines again to confirm their arrival times.

"Alright, already," Jeter huffed and puffed, blowing air through his mouth like a fish out of water. "Just do something, Aggie -- anything" He faced Bandit. "That's what I get for not hiring Ki Toy who is in Atlanta. Could've put her in an envelope and mailed her, that's how close she is"

After a minute, the white woman, Aggie timidly approached. "I'm sorry, Mr. Jeter, but that flight will be delayed. It took off late"

"Not again," Jeter yelped. "Fucking airlines. Don't they know that time is fucking money" When he finished venting his frustration and realized Agnes 'Aggie' Bowman was still standing there, he fumed. "Is there anything else, Aggie?"

"I have a slight suggestion, Mr. Jeter"

"You do, do you? Let's hear it"

"Why don't we just shoot some stills, using just the men since they are already here. You know, do some walk-throughs so the guys can get familiar with the shoot layout"

"Would you?" Jeter looked squarely at Bandit. "That would help so much. Personally, I didn't want to suggest it, but we could get some camera time in before the divas arrive. Please"

"C'mon, man, let's do it" Bandit sighed. He wanted to get this shit over with. "Set your gear up"

"It's already set up. All we need is you guys"

"Where's Shine?", Bandit asked turning to Justice.

Oh, you'll see him in a minute. He getting ready"

A great sense of relief surged through Bandit's body when he was ushered into the living room of the mansion and saw that it was actually set up for a video shoot, but the feeling didn't last.

"LIE FACE DOWN ON THE GODDAMN FLOOR!" a voice thundered and before they clearly understood what was going down, Bandit and his crew were completely surrounded by both men and women with automatic weapons. "GET DOWN! NOW!"

For a long while Justice didn't say a word. He seemed absolutely content merely to watch the event unfold before his eyes. This was a major triumph for him.

"What is this all about, Justice?" Bandit demanded to know as his hands were cuffed behind his back. "What the fuck is wrong with you?"

"As if you didn't know," Justice remarked caustically. "You set a good trap, dawg, but you used the wrong bait. Anyway, we got up on you niggas just in time" Justice pointed at Bandit. "Bring him and three more in the guest bedroom. Take the rest to the spot"

The bedroom had been prepared. Four chairs were arranged in front of a TV monitor with camera attachments.

"Sit 'em down"

Bandit and the three other thugs were roughly shoved into the chairs by four of Justice's men who were masked. Each man held a gun.

CRUNK

"Roll the camera," Justice said from off-screen. His voice faded for a second, then returned. "Greetings, KoKo. This is payback. You murdered four of our soldiers. Now these four men of yours will die" Justice laughed. "Now this is reality TV!"

The package was shipped overnight express and the next morning when KoKo signed for it, he carefully examined the alloy and plastic protective slipcover it had come in. Though K C Complex received, on average, dozens of priority mailings a month, this one made him highly suspicious. The fact that it had been mailed from Virginia Beach was also a bad omen because Bandit would have called first before mailing him a package and chances were good that Bandit, if he chose to use the mail, would have used his home address rather than the more public one at the K C Complex.

KoKo took a big gulp of air and then retired to his spacious corner office where he put in the video. It crackled to life, but initially there was nothing but a blank, blue screen and a voiceover.

"The first and most important thing to understand," the voice announced, "is that you have no win. My name is Rah-Rah and I will crush you if you do not comply with my wishes", Rah-Rah paused.

"You have, as you will see shortly, just suffered a terrible setback, but you will learn to adjust. I was indeed a lot less brutal than I could have been given my total control over the situation, but your men died painlessly"

KoKo felt faint. The screen flickered and a crystal clear image of Bandit and three other of his Westside Connection appeared. KoKo saw the four masked men behind them and he quickly looked off, tears in his eyes. "You might find this interesting," the narrator on the video snarled, his voice both menacing and triumphant. "One man. One slug"

KoKo wanted to scream as he witnessed the murder of his best friend Bandit. KoKo put his hand over his heart as though that gesture would stop the pain. Then he broke down in tears.

The screen switched images again. This time a background with a map of the South appeared and the disengaged voice of Rah-Rah filled the room.

"Want some more, KoKo or do we call it even and come to term?" Rah-Rah's voice was clear, his diction perfect. "Do not resist me and you can share in this vision of mine. What I propose is an alliance between me and you. Together we can rule the world. As a team, we can make history but the decision is yours because I will triumph either with or without you. I know that you are filled with both pain and rage and I understand that, but this is not the time to let your emotions run away with you. Trust me, KoKo, this is not an experiment. I know exactly what I'm doing and I will succeed. Do not resist me. Surrender"

Rah-Rah rambled on for a few more minutes about his vision and how he planned to unify all thugs under one rule, how this would help eliminate all the senseless violence, and how it was his destiny to accomplish this mission.

"Now that I'm in VA, watch how quickly the hoods come into my grasp. I intend to smother VA within a matter of days, bodies will fill the streets, and then guess what, NC will be next. Ask yourself, KoKo, do you want war or do you want money? Think about that. Now as for your other six men, they are still alive and well. If you want to get down with me, I will release them unharmed. Otherwise, I will massacre them. To contact me, use the e-mail address that will appear at the bottom of the screen. I await your instant response. Goodbye"

Without delay KoKo flicked ON his computer. He thought for a brief second, then replied.

"KILL THEM!"

Shine and Janeen sat under a candy-striped umbrella on the beach in Brazil. They were talking and laughing as they sipped Pina Coladas. Janeen, as usual, looked adorable, the two piece bathing suit was hugging her body like a second layer of skin.

Shine loved this ho.

He had no idea if he had been wrong or not about getting out of VA, but the block was hot and it was only a matter of time before guns were blazing. Anyway, he had done his part. He had earned his keep, even though he had played both ends from the middle, but who the fuck had said anything about sticking around to witness the powder keg blowing up.

Shit, he would much rather be out on the beach with Janeen than watching niggas shoot at one another. And that was why he had split. And deep down inside, he had the feeling that it was the best decision of his life.

Rah-Rah was madder than a motherfucka!

The 10 bodies were shipped to Charlotte.

Chapter 11

With nothing to guide him but the Crunk, KoKo blasted the Yin Yang Twins to almost maximum volume and at the end to his fourth drink, the raspy, grating voices sounded almost angelic. KoKo vowed to destroy Rah-Rah.

Motherfucka had plundered him! In any way, the ultimate defeat was the loss of your soldiers and all of his dead comrades had been true thug warriors, but now they were gone, lost to this world forever. No more pussy. No more paper. No more weed. R.I.P.

War was such a mysterious biz'ness and KoKo bowed his head in remembrance of the thugs who had just fallen in the line of duty. KoKo had always believed himself to be a master of strategy until Rah-Rah had totally out-maneuvered him, hitting him where it hurt most. And it had hurt.

KoKo knew that weed and whiskey were not going to bring his boys back, but smoking and drinking did help to lift his spirits. Oh how he wished he could revive the soldiers of the Westside Connection, but he knew he had been stripped of them until the end of time. "Goddammit!", he screamed aloud.

He turned the music up.

Rah-Rah knew that KoKo was the only one in the South who stood a limited chance against him now that he had a temporary alliance with the other 4 boroughs of New York. Together as a team, they had the numbers, the heart, and the firepower to take the entire South, and with a base in VA from which to headquarter there was nothing that could stop him. He would come thundering out of Virginia Beach like the northwind and would blow everybody away who got in his path.

Moses London had been listening intently. "You can do a lot of killing that way, have niggas dropping like gnats but when a killer stares blindly into his own gunsmoke he'll start to miss his target, see what I'm sayin' Rah-Rah? Fighting is about capability, not the caliber of your piece. Motherfucka get the jump on you, you gonna get your ass in the wind even though you toting a cannon in your pocket, so don't brush this shit off and think you can live off of your so-called intimidation factor"

"But why won't that work if we start hitting 'em and then keep right on hitting 'em?"

"Because, young fool, you gonna be getting hit too and shit will break down mighty goddamn quick if you boys begin to believe that you willing to just sacrifice them. That happens, your ass is through booking and you know why? Treachery, that's why. A motherfucka will turn on you in a heartbeat if he see where you ain't got his ass covered no mo' and in a war, Rah, the only thing worse than a bullet from your enemy is a knife in the back from one of your own troopers"

As Moses London spoke, Rah-Rah tried to picture what he was making mention of but he couldn't see any of his people getting weak on him. He didn't feel, however, like telling that to Moses. The old hit man was too shrewd not to miss an occasion to point out the flaws of that point of view, so Rah-Rah kept quiet. It was probably much better to just sit quietly and listen.

Back in the days, Moses was a local legend in Harlem who had once single-handedly drove off an attack by the police department who had come to arrest his partner, Rah-Rah's father. Needless to say, no arrests were made that night.

"Niggas in the South, they're different from us" Moses considered how best to explain that observation. "But they're still niggas and niggas anywhere are a menace to something or someone even if they just got to be a pest to themselves, but in the South the underworld was not built on violence. Now that don't mean the niggas punks or nothing, but that shuck and jive about southern hospitality ain't no shuck and jive. Motherfuckas play the game like true gentlemen. Why you think all the best con men come out of the bottom?"

Rah-Rah shrugged. "Why?"

"Niggas like a vulture, can sit on a lick until it's ripe. Nigga up North lack that type patience so he play the ruff-off game, just ruff shit off. Niggas down South will sweat shit out. Guess that's because they had to learn to play the white man real smooth, couldn't talk back or ruff shit off from him so they had to have a Plan B which was to revise that of head-scratching, foot shuffling Uncle Tom bullshit into game. Nigga did it too"

"But what that got to do with right now?"

"Rah, think" Moses shook his head slowly. "It's not easy to whop a motherfucka with patience and that's your lesson for today.

"C'mon, Moses, damn, I'm just trying to run shit past you so I can get some feedback"

Moses relaxed. "If you weren't my godson, I'd let your ass right into a nightmare? You inherited Harlem. Ain't it good enough for you?"

So that was it. Moses thought that Rah-Rap's plans were based on getting up out of Harlem completely, but that was not wholly accurate. Rah-Rah knew that while Moses might not knock his plans out loud, he realized that the old head would consider it a slight if Harlem was put up for grabs. Harlem, no matter what, was meant to be run by the Tillman family forever.

"I would never desert Harlem"

"Your roots run deep here, so don't cheat Rah 3 out of his chance to be The King of New York" Moses glanced at Rah-Rah, his eyes showing concern. "I guess you gotta do what you gotta do, but don't let your dirty little war mark Harlem for death"

"Never that, Moses. You ain't gotta worry. I promise"

Moses' voice changed. "To win Rah, you gonna have to be versatile in your tactics and strategy"

"Why not just blitz 'em?"

"'Cause it'll get your fool ass wiped out"

"Okay, okay, forget that then. What do you suggest?"

"That you learn some motherfucking geography. And a little history won't hurt" Moses sighed. "Look at a house, Rah. It's a house, but you got different rooms in it, goddammit. You got a bathroom, you got a kitchen, you got bedrooms, dens, other rooms, all of 'em different. Same way with the South. You got cities and like the rooms in a crib, they all different with their own functions, and for the same reason you wouldn't shit in the middle of your kitchen you can't fuck with the South without understanding the style and function of each major city you plan to hit"

"I figure I got to fuck up some shit in VA, Memphis, Charlotte, and Atlanta"

"Fire up that blunt while I think for a minute. You picked the right ones, baby" After Moses hit the weed, he sat back and gazed at the wispy smoke spiraling up to the ceiling. "You picked the right ones, baby," he repeated.

"I think you've already told me that", Rah-Rah protested. "What's the strategy?"

Moses sat up in the chair quickly, looking as if he was ready to invoke the devil by some ancient incantation. "Nigga, you better listen carefully 'cause this is the key to your strategy"

"I'm listening," Rah-Rah said excitedly. "Spit it"

"You gonna have to collapse VA, wreck Memphis, but you gonna have to attack Charlotte"

"What about the ATL?"

Moses smiled. "I might can get you a pass in Atlanta"

Rah-Rah's eyes brightened. "For real?!"

"And you better be glad cause you don't need to be fucking with them crazy niggas in Hotlanta. Niggas got teflon hearts, don't care if the sun don't never shine no mo'"

"Niggas can't be that dangerous"

"I hate to think they ain't," Moses objected. "Niggas ain't normal. Plus they be operating under the damn influence of that Crunk music. Don't you laugh, Rah. The thugs down there live off Crunk like most niggas live off oxygen"

"And Crunk is what makes them hard?" Rah-Rah looked at Moses crazily. "But Crunk is music"

"Try telling that to them niggas down there.. They be feeling Lil' Jon just like Hitler was feeling Wagner. When Hitler went up against the whole world, he used to listen to Wagner because the music inspired him, made him confident He could kick the whole world's ass. It made him not to be scared of shit", Moses sat on the edge of his chair. "You saw that movie Brave Heart, didn't you?"

"Yeah," Rah-Rah admitted, "Mel Gibson flick"

"Okay, what did the Scottish warriors do when they got ready to go into battle? They played those Bagpipes, remember? That shit get 'em crunk up and they fight like a motherfucka. You seen it. Shit, look at our own folks, the Africans. They get psyched for war by beating on their drums and once the sound gets down into their soul, it's on"

Rah-Rah thought it over. "And Crunk is war music"

"For them ATL niggas, yeah. You ever listen to any Crunk?"

"Naw, ain't my thang"

"Then you better make it your damn thang, young, fool ass nigga. And while you at it, buy you some Wagner. Both Crunk and Wagner possess the same type of martial power. Make a motherfucka put his back against the wall with a chest puffed up with I-don't-give-a-damn, and you got your goddamn hands full, see what I'm saying, Rah?"

"But you say you can get me a free pass with them stupid niggas, didn't you?" Suddenly Rah-Rah didn't want to jump in the ATL's shit. "How I go about-------"

"Leave that up to me. I'm cool with an old playa down there named Thin Man. I'll holla"

"Thanks, Mo"

"No problem, but Rah don't start grinning like the cat that ate the canary because even with Atlanta on the sidelines, it won't be easy. Them Charlotte niggas gonna bang with you to the death and you know why?"

"You tell me"

"Niggas ain't got no face, see what I'm saying so they trying to rep. Tell me, who done heard of Charlotte? Spot might as well be on the moon. Everybody in the world know about Atlanta, and back in the glory days when niggas was Mackin', some of the best hoes in the country came out of Memphis. A pimp wasn't top shelf unless he had at least one ho in his stable from Memphis. Niggas from everywhere used to flock to Memphis because the word about the *city* was that the women loved hoeing. That's how Memphis got it's rep, but some hellified pimps came out of the city also. Memphis was like the Pimp Capitol of America and all the niggas who were out and about on both coasts were hip to that fact"

Rah-Rah got the picture. "And like right now, Missy Elliott, Timbaland and that crew got all eyes on VA"

"But what is Charlotte, now or then, known for in the thug world?"

"Nothing, that I know of?"

"And you're right. Niggas down there ain't known for shit. They ain't got no face, so fucking your ass up will give them mad props and that's why the motherfuckas will prove to be so dangerous. Charlotte looking for face, Rah-Rah, so don't fuck up and let them niggas snatch yours"

Chapter 12

"Long time, no see"

Moses grunted, his attention on the stripper on stage. "Tell me something, Thin Man, when we were young, did bitches legs grow that long ?"

"No siree and their asses didn't get that big either. Must be that formula milk the government feeding these children because goddamn these young gals be filled up at twelve, just waiting to get ripe so they can start on a new generation of gals with even bigger tails"

"Whoo-weee," Moses chanted, "what she trying to do, break something? And oh shit, what was that-------poetry in motion? Damn, young bitch, don't be so mean"

Thin Man and Moses were both on their second drink.

"A few more of these and somebody gonna have to call the fire department to come dig us out"

Moses said nothing.

The Blue Flame was a paradise of exposed flesh and pornographic display where patrons found it hard to resist crowding the stage when the dance divas performed their rhythms of life. Most of the regulars argued the point heatedly that this spot could match hoes with any of the top strip clubs in the area including Magic City and Pin-ups. In fact, the locals swore you could damn near taste pussy in the air at The Blue Flame.

"So what's broken?"

Moses was puffing on a Newport, still staring at the dancer on stage, he turned toward Thin Man. "I need a free pass" Moses' hand trembled slightly. "It's a big favor"

"Tell me more"

The trembling stopped as Moses took another drag, then blew smoke rings at the ceiling. "You heard anything about a war between thugs?"

Thin Man played dumb. "What else do these young thugs know but war. Just yesterday, a little girl got caught in the crossfire of two rival thug groups. The-------"

"Naw, bigger than that, I mean"

"Okay" Thin Man shrugged nonchalantly. "So what if I have heard? What's it to you , old friend?"

"My godson is involved" Moses stared hard at his old partner.

"So is mine" Thin Man held the gaze.

Finding no reason to break the stare-down, both the old heads continued to look through each other until they figured one thing could possibly lead to another and neither desired to even talk or think about that. They looked away.

"Who your godson?"

"A kid named Tillman"

"Tillman? Wouldn't happen to be Rah-Rah's son, would it? Them the only Tillmans I know that comes to mind"

"Yep. Kid named Rah-Rah too, just like his old man. Who you godfather to?"

"Nobody you know, but the kid down home"

"This calls for a goddamn drink. Just goes to show how small the world is"

"And how crazy," Thin Man added.

After the drinks arrived it was terribly difficult to waste away the rest of the night on bullshit from the past especially now that future shit threatened to rip apart their friendship.

"I guess it goes without saying, but just between us I can't do nothing for you if you hunting for a backdoor man. I can't let you ease in down here on my godson" Thin Man voice dropped. "I know you can understand that"

Moses stuck out his fist for some dap. "I understand and I have to accept that. No problem, but I gotta ask. I mean, you ain't gotta answer if you don't want to, but is Atlanta rolling out or staying out, neutral, I mean.

Thin Man shook his head. "You know I can't call that, Mo"

"Just asking, my man, just asking"

"What now?"

"Shit, nothing now. I came, I asked, I did my bit for my godson and though I shot a blank, my conscience is clear" Moses took one, final look at the dancer, then took a deep breath. "Walk me out to my ride and show me how to get back to the highway and I'm gone"

"Want another drink for the road?"

"Naw, better not. Got a long drive in front of me"

Both men stood to leave.

"Glad you understand, Mo"

"Shit, I might end up thanking you before this is over" Moses grinned slyly. "Every time one of those young thugs

135

from Harlem bite the dust I get to serve them so my cash register gonna be going KA-CHING!"

Once the old heads had gotten outside, they both could still hear the loud music ringing in their ears.

"Oh yeah, have you gained weight?" Moses studied his old friend. You look like you have"

They walked on.

Man, I'm the same waist size, a 30, that I was back in the days. 30 in the waist, pretty in the face" Thin Man stopped. "Now, you might be don' added about a good twenty pounds since I first met you. Remember that?"

"The Ali/Quarry fight"

"Naw, man", Thin man corrected, "it wasn't at the fight. It was after the fight at the party at Chicken Man's"

"Still was almost thirty-five years ago"

Thin Man let out his breath slowly. "Damn, partner, where does all the time go"

"I don't know where it goes, Thin Man, but I do know that yours just ran out"

Thin Man stared in disbelief at the gun in Moses' hand. "C'mon, Mo"

"C'mon, my ass, nigga. This is what you get from being out of touch. I still don't take no for an answer. I'm still the Undertaker, so Rest In Peace, Thin Man"

Back at his hotel, Moses used the pay phone in the lobby to call New York. His nerves were still tingling as he waited on Rah-Rah to pick up. Thin Man had been his first kill in a long, long time and it had him juiced up. That one gunshot had just changed things. Killing for him had just become more than a philosophy. It was once again a way of life for him and though he didn't want to admit it, he didn't mind the change.

"Yo"

"It's Mo"

"How did it go, Godfather?"

"Not as good as I had hoped, but everything is now open to re-negotiation. You see my man, Thin Man, was on the wrong side of the ball, but he sleep now so all his bets are off. So now, I go on the offensive"

Moses had faith that Gemini would give in. He just didn't know when although he had no intentions to keep splitting hairs with the nigga.

Moses shook his head. "The primary objective, you keep forgetting, is that I want this to happen and I say once more that it would benefit you greatly if you got behind New York and help my peeps handle this little bit of a problem they have down here"

"But Thin Man--------"

"Everything has changed. Thin Man is no longer alive to give a damn about what happens anywhere in the world so you can stop looking for him to pull you through" Moses was standing tall, his legs tight, his arms hanging loosely at his side like a F.O.I. member in The Nation of Islam. "I'm gonna let you in on a well kept secret which is this. You either join New York of die" Moses could read the expression of fear on Gemini's face, but there still wasn't any sign of a breakthrough. "I had hoped that I wouldn't have to appeal to you in such an unbrotherly way, but we're grown men so why bullshit, huh?"

"The ATL ain't got no beef-------"

"Look, forget the shit about who got a beef with who because when you get right down to it, this ain't about beef. It's about reconstruction" Moses folded his arms across his chest. "New York is going to reconstruct the South. We're already on the move and pretty soon VA is going to get ambushed. It ain't gonna be a sweet sight and if we gotta pile the bodies up like sandbags to let you motherfuckas know we not playing, then that's just what we'll do. We got plans to devastate you southen niggas, except this city, so that's why we offering you this partnership" Moses took a step, closing the small gap between him and Gemini. "You either take this deal or we make you eat your dead"

It was a done deal.

Moses knew better than to try that same shit on Hercules Parker who was next on his visiting list of Atlanta thugs. In fact, the possibility of anyone either scaring of intimidating Hercules was virtually non-existent. Motherfucka had ice in his veins.

When Moses showed up at the car detailing shop where Hercules had instructed him to come, he was instantly inspected by a thin sista with caramel skin and braided hair. When she was satisfied that Moses was a legit visitor, she pressed a button hidden under the counter and pointed to a door.

"Go through there"

Stepping inside the door, Moses found himself trapped between four walls with nowhere to go. In about a second, he heard the almost inaudible gnashing of gears and to his utter amazement the wall panel to his right split smoothly, hissing open like the doors on and elevator. Moses stepped through, noticing the tiny camera for the first time. It was lodged in a corner of the ceiling.

Clearing the opening Moses stepped into what appeared to be a break room or game room of some sort. Maybe this is where employees came for lunch or during breaks. However now, it was empty. Completely.

Moses walked to a pool table and picked up a stick, broke the balls and sunk a few balls before two men entered from another sliding door entrance.

"You any good?" Hercules asked casually. "Got time for a game?"

"Naw, my biz'ness too important to be put off. Sorry. Maybe some other time"

"C'mon, let's have a sit-down" When Moses glanced at the third man in the room, Hercules smiled. "My brother, he cool. Plus, he call shots when I'm off somewhere getting my dick sucked"

Moses took a quick second to look the brothers over. Both were sneaker pimps. Hercules sported a pair of Phat Farm kicks customized by D.D. And A.I., two dudes from Brooklyn while his little brother (if 6' 1", 210 could be deemed small) wore a pair of tricked-out Nikes. They both had their massive upper bodies covered in Limited Edition Lot 29 shirts with Elmer Fudd in a military helmet on the front. Cute, Moses thought.

In turn, the brothers watched Moses and though it was unspoken their bemused expression said it loud and clear. While the brothers would accord Moses props as an O.G., in all honesty they felt he belonged to an alien species of hustlers where slow money/sho' money was the name of the game. In today's fast money/cash money thug world, O.G.'s were dead weight and most young playas wished they would retire or step aside. Old niggas just weren't a part of it anymore.

"Holla, O.G" Hercules prompted.

As Moses spoke, he was careful not to say anything that would put his case at a disadvantage, so for a moment he talked with extreme caution, but once he had glossed over the main points, he free-styled saying whatever the fuck would get the brothers' attention.

"They punks if they surrender in VA," Hercules acknowledged blandly. "Motherfuckas from nowhere in the world better not come to the ATL with no plans like that. We ain't never scared"

"And that's why we chose to deal with Atlanta as a partner instead of as a foe"

"You did right, O.G. 'cause we ain't wit' nobody punking us"

"That's correct" Hercules added. "We check niggas, not get checked"

"And that's understood all over the country. Thugs far and wide know ATL will go off if they get stepped to and to be totally on the real, New York is not interested in coming at you with no drama. Up Top, all we got is much love and big ups to this city. We respect the fact that y'all dangerous"

"Still, them VA niggas will diss the whole South if they give up the pussy without a fight. Motherf*****"

"Chill, Samson," Hercules admonished his brother, "VA gotta live or die by they own swords"

"But it's the whole South they after"

"No, we do not want Atlanta," Moses interjected. "I emphasize that. We have no interest in the ATL except to be allies," Moses sounded weary. "Y'all dangerous"

"And you know why we dangerous?", Samson snarled. "We mean because we mongrels. We like a pit bull mixed with a rotweiller" Samson's eyes blazed. "That's right O.G., we the new hybrid southern baller, a deadly mix of motherfucka and thug. Look at me and my brother. You ain't seeing what you think you seeing 'cause you ain't seeing just ATL. You seeing

ATL plus. Pops was from Philly. Moms from out in L.A. They bump heads down heah-------and POW! You got the re-mix. And that's how it is all over this city. Ain't nobody originally from heah. Motherfuckas heah 'cause they trying to get away from something or someone back on the home court, O.G. This city the Black Mecca so you get bitches from Jersey making babies with niggas from out of Detroit or you got niggas from D.C. Fucking hoes from Chicago. And all the while you got all these lil' nappy-headed re-mix kids. Mongrel motherfuckas we might be, but guess what, O.G., we be repping ATL" Samson pounded his thick chest. "We don't know shit bout where Moms from or where Pops from, but we got ATL in our hearts, you feel me, O.G.. And that's why we so goddamn dangerous"

The conversation stopped abruptly as though Samson had lost interest, but when Hercules gave him some dap, Moses could sense he was on the verge of launching into another tirade.

"Look, y'all, New York is a friend and all we ask from ATL is that you let us use your city as a base of operations. We don't want you to lift one finger to assist us. We just need a spot where we can sandwich Charlotte from. We already got VA and if ATL will honor our request, New York will have Charlotte in a pincher move, caught between our soldiers up top and down below"

"That's very clever," Hercules confessed, "but what do we get out of this for our generosity?"

"We'll divide South Carolina with you. Give you Columbia and Charleston"

"We like Charlotte better"

That response caught Moses off guard.

"You got a problem with that, O.G.?", Hercules quizzed.

Moses cast a wary glance at the brothers. "Depends on why you want it"

Without wanting to go into a lot of details over his concerns, Moses knew that letting Charlotte fall into the hands of Atlanta wasn't something that would go over big with New York because the last thing the North needed was for these two powerhouses to merge and come together. Moses knew for certain that Charlotte would immediately go into the business of trying to convince Atlanta to go back into combat with them to avenge their defeat and for that reason alone Moses could never cede Charlotte to Atlanta. No goddamn way.

"I don't see where that concern you, O.G.," Samson snarled, "but Charlotte has been jocking ATL for decades now, riding our dicks and we need to break these bitches of the habit. Motherfuckas even trying to look like us. For real, look at they skyline and look at ours. A nigga can't tell who's who"

Moses wasn't buying it. "And that's it?"

"Like I said, it ain't none of your biz'ness"

"I say it is"

"Cool it y'all," Hercules demanded. "Let me say this. My brother is right. We want Charlotte, the reason being that in a minute it's gonna turn into a Cinderella and we need to move in while shit still on the DL. The ATL getting congested with niggas and Charlotte 'bout to be the best spot to ride out to. Charlotte will give us more breathing space, more living room"

"I-I don't know about that," Moses said unsteadily. "I promise you two cities in South Carolina which would be closer and more convenient. Plus, you can have any two cities in VA. These two spots you can use like for hang-outs, a joint where you can go to vacation, or party or just to fuck some stray hoes. You see what I'm saying?"

"Charlene!" Hercules yelled and a beautiful light-skinned sista with green eyes walked through the sliding door.

"Yes," she responded.

"Go with homeboy. Take him out to Gladys Knight's Chicken & Waffles, give him some pussy, take him out to Greenbriar Mall. Just entertain him until we hit you on your celly and tell you to bring his ass back"

"C'mon, Big Boy," Charlene said sweetly. "I don't bite"

"That pussy does though," Samson winked. "I advise you to hit it"

"We just need time to think shit over, know what I mean?" Hercules placed a hand reassuringly on Moses' shoulder. "A good biz'nessman always studies all his options before making a decision this big"

"Plus we giving you enough time to get a shot of the best ass in the city. The head smokin' too. I strongly urge you to go out and buy yourself a 6-pack of them ol' Viagra pills and get busy"

"Let's go, honey" Moses reached for Charlene's hand. Stepping back through the sliding doors, Moses stopped, then spoke calmly to Hercules. "Study long, study wrong"

"We'll holla"

"Yeah, O.G.," Samson grinned, "we got this heah. You need to go 'head on and holla at that pussy"

"It's handled, young ass niggas. Bet that"

Charlene smiled.

Chapter 13

IT WAS ON!

After several minutes of sustained gunfire on Virginia Beach Boulevard, the New York crew pushed into Ingleside, a housing project where the VA thugs were trying to make a stand. New York had just crushed a small pocket of resistance from VA niggas who had mobbed up at the Casablanca, using it as a fortress, fighting only sporadically in the hopes of holding off the advancing North until reinforcements from Norfolk and Portsmouth could arrive. That was a bad plan.

Justice recognized instantly that he could not afford to battle on two fronts simultaneously so he had signaled for his contingent from Queens to stop trading bullets with Casablanca and to storm the joint and then to burn it to the ground. That was a good plan.

Now, with this new uprising just around the corner, Justice knew that he had only a few more minutes of good fighting time before the police came and that would pose a second problem. Already, he acknowledged that it would be much more difficult to subdue Ingleside than it had the Casablanca. For once, Justice knew that VA would take the offensive and immediately instigate a guerrilla-type hit and run attack against him which would be a legitimate tactic as it would force New York to get out of their rides and to give fight on foot which is what VA wanted. In the dark and on foot, New York would get wiped out in seconds.

Knowing time was not on his side tonight, Justice called for one final frontal assault which he himself would lead. Quickly assembling the remnants of the New York forces from off Princess Anne Road where acrid black smoke still clung to the Casablanca, Justice stormed Ingleside but withdrew almost as quickly. The police sirens were too close.

New York pulled back, disappearing into the VA night back up to Timbaland's crib which they had commandeered. Justice cursed his bad luck. He coulda took them niggas!

The phone call jarred KoKo awake.

"It's on, nigga. Protect your neck"

KoKo knew who the caller was. Rah-Rah.

Sitting cross-legged in the bed, KoKo shook Kendra awake. "Wake up, babe, gotta help me work the phone"

"What's up, KoKo?", Kendra panted. "Is it, is it New York?"

"Yeah, I think they might be moving. Gotta find out for real" KoKo tossed her some telephone numbers. "Hit those niggas, tell them you my woman, and ask what's up. I'll call up some other numbers"

Kendra looked up, fear in her eyes. "What if New York is moving?"

KoKo sighed. "That means the Thug Civil War is on and that we gotta hit them niggas hard and quick"

Kendra started dialing. So did KoKo.

"It's on!" Coot screamed in KoKo's ear. "New York motherfuckas on the march. They ain't bullshitting"

"How bad?"

"Ten confirmed kills so far. Ain't no telling how many bodies gonna pop up when it gets daylight"

There was a slight pause. "I guess this is really it, huh, Coot? A civil war between thugs"

"Seems like it, homeboy, so how Carolina gonna roll? You know you The General, so you gotta make the call"

"Right now, let VA handle it, but if them niggas soldier it out we'll send some troopers up to help them hold the fort down, but everybody looking for them niggas to fold so I ain't gonna risk sending our people up not knowing how much fight VA got in 'em"

"So what we do?"

"Prepare and put together a battle plan, that's what"

Coot sighed, "New York gonna fuck them niggas up bad"

"Look, brer, I know what you feeling, but we gotta get Carolina in order or else they'll fuck us up too. This shit real, so keep on top of what's happening. Hit me anytime, okay?"

"Yeah, man, you got it. Out"

Suddenly KoKo got the impression that VA was going to fall quickly which meant that NC would be next up which also meant that New York would be on top of them in a heartbeat because as long as they could deal with the South on a state-by-state basis, the momentum would belong to the invaders. Somehow, KoKo had to unite the whole South, however his intuition told him not to count on either VA or Atlanta. Support from either would be delusion, but just the same KoKo knew that he couldn't just let New York continue to select their own targets. If the South was going to have a future or if the southern thug culture was going to survive, he was going to have to take the battle to them niggas from up top. No ifs, ands, or buts about it.

KoKo speed dialed Coot.

"Yo"

"Get VA on the line. Tell them Carolina got they back. We on the way. Round up-------"

"Ain't a good idea. KoKo," Coot groaned miserably. "Not good at fucking all"

"What's up? Don't tell me VA done threw in the towel this early"

"Naw, Ko, it ain't that. VA still scuffling like champs"

"Then why can't we roll in. Ain't that what you want?"

"It was"

"Damn, Coot, now you ain't making sense.   If VA holding strong, why can't we roll in and take up the slack?"

"Because them ATL niggas don' let New York in. If we so much as move a toenail, they can slide right in the backdoor on Charlotte. So we stuck 'cause motherfuckas made a power move. As long as they in Atlanta we gotta stay posted up in case they start some shit from the rear. You feel that?"

KoKo hung up without saying goodbye. He just let the damn phone fall to the carpet. He made an effort to mask his fear so that his woman would not pick up on just how much energy he had lost, especially since it was customary of him to let her see that he was always in charge.

But for the second time Rah-Rah had out-maneuvered him, beating him to the punch and for the first time KoKo could vaguely perceive what the niggas up top had in store for him. Rah-Rah had anticipated that Charlotte would rust off to prop VA up when the shit got hot up there, so to neutralize that move he set up shop on Charlotte's tail, tying Charlotte's hands because if KoKo moved an inch, it would expose Carolina's flank to a hit from the bottom.

"Call my godfather," KoKo told Kendra.

At least five more VA thugs were slaughtered within minutes of the 4:00 a.m. sneak attack when New York resumed its hit on Ingleside. Since the streets were empty, Justice and his boys operated on foot, practically going door to door offering financial rewards to anyone who helped pinpoint the location of the thug stronghold in the community, and killing those who resisted.

On some streets, New York encountered nothing or no one while on others, gunfire erupted, but it was mostly small-arms fire until Justice tried to head back out of the hood. There he met heavier artillery.

Justice lost three men coming out of the projects. Two more were wounded, neither seriously as New York was caught off guard and surprised by VA thugs who had secured the street where the New York getaway cars were parked. The whips had already been torched.

Isolated from their escape vehicles and on alien turf, many of the New York team thought the end was near for them as VA closed in on them from all sides. New York was trapped.

Justice saw that there was nothing left to do but pull up and run, so giving the order to retreat Justice and his boys broke camp amid a hail of bullets. Down one street, up another, through a yard, all the while zig-zagging, hoping to dodge the fire at their backs.

VA closed in quickly. They knew the neighborhood so they moved to cut off all exits while New York ran faster, trying to put distance between them and the niggas chasing

149

them. The hot southern air, thick with humidity, stank with blood and sweat but as Justice turned a corner he saw what he felt might save New York, so he quickly stationed his men into positions as Jaheim and Sharmek expertly hot-wired four cars.

Justice felt his body swimming in sweat, his clothes plastered to his skin, his eyes stinging, but on the surface he was cool as he blasted away at VA who had taken up battle stations down the block.

Cries rent the night as lead tore into the flesh of men on both sides of the street. Death was on the corner.

Let's go!" Jaheim shouted. The cars were ready.

Piling hurried into the stolen rides, the breath compressed into their lungs, New York blazed up the streets as VA shot at them wildly. A stray bullet hit Zee in the nape of the neck, rupturing his jugular. He died in Justice's arm.

War was hell!

Over the years, Charlotte, North Carolina and Rock Hill, South Carolina had both struggled for control of a valuable strip of turf on the border that separated the two cities, so there was always bad blood between them. However KoKo hoped that the current crisis would link them up, allowing them to look beyond the tensions of the past. If not, KoKo would deal with them later.

After a brief council session among themselves, Tony Rome appointed himself as spokesman for the SC-group and spoke directly to KoKo.

"Our allegiance is not up for sale" he began, "so both your money and your begging are worthless. We will either support you or we won't , everything depending on how the fuck we feel about the shit that's going down"

KoKo didn't like the way this was heading. But he tried not to let the distaste show on his face. He listened.

Speaking more boldly now, Tony Rome said, "No one dictates to us. No one tells us shit. We answer to no one"

"I hate to interrupt you, Tony, but man, it's unbelievable that we can't get our shit together when it's do or die time. Brer, if we don't support each other, then we doomed. Look at what happened to the South during the first Civil War"

"Fuck history," Tony Rome, a short, brown-skinned brotha spat, "this ain't about no crackers. This a nigga war"

"But what you fail to realize is that disunity knows no color and it will fuck a nigga up just like it fucked the white boys up and since you talk about fucking history, I say that we better not let history fuck us," KoKo frowned, "did you know that before the Independence War there was no North or South Carolina. It was just Carolina. But what happened is that Carolina couldn't decide who to support. They didn't know whether to fight for America or to fight for England and the shit had them so fucked up that they divided into two states. I hope this shit don't divide us so that we forget that we are one"

"I ain't tripping," Tony Rome chuckled mirthlessly, "but ain't it a bitch how unity so important now that it's so convenient for you Charlotte niggas"

"Why it gotta just be so important to Charlotte. This is a Southern issue. Why you can't see that?"

"Because I don't and you know what else? Fuck Charlotte. We ain't in, nigga"

KoKo wasn't particularly surprised by that response, "Then there's this other issue we gotta deal with"

"Which is?"

"Since you not going to watch the backdoor, does that mean you gonna roll in with them niggas when they come. Do y'all hate us that much?"

Tony Rome seemed amused. "I was afraid you was going to ask that"

"And the answer is?"

"You'll find out when the time comes" Tony Rome nodded at two of his boys. "Jay. Ben. Please escort our guest to his whip and across the state line" Then he confronted KoKo. "Have a nice war, my nigga"

KoKo stood, stiff and intense. "Man, I'm telling you, I better not see none of y'all niggas in Charlotte with New York or I'll--------"

"Nigga, shut the fuck up, and go" Tony Rome had yanked out a Sig Sauer and in a flash had it behind KoKo's ear. "You don't make policy down here, motherfucka. We move Rock Hill style and I think that over the years you done got some idea of how we do it, so if you don't wanna make me make you get some religion, I advise you to get on the road and don't look back" He removed the gun. "Bye"

KoKo's eye's grew cold, but he said nothing. Then he left.

That was stupid of them. Though Tony Rome and Rock Hill repulsed the initial attack by Charlotte, within 30 seconds of steady gunfire, KoKo was right up on top of them.

KoKo squeezed through the door, emptied the clip of both his 9s and then whipped out his assault rifle. He caught Ben, Tony Rome's right hand man, in the back of the head with a quick burst from the AK and working the gun in a tight, winging arc, he hit Jay in the ass as the man was attempting to hoist himself through a trap door in the ceiling.

It was over that quick.

Resting for a moment to catch his breath KoKo instructed that Tony Rome and all his boys be rounded up and brought before him, and sensing that the house was no longer dangerous KoKo relaxed, but had to restrain the impulse to put a bullet through Tony Rome's head when the leader of the Rock Hill posse was escorted into the room. He pointed the gun at Tony Rome.

"We didn't start out like this, Tony," KoKo growled angrily. "This ain't for us Carolina Dawgs" He nodded his head towards the door. "That goddamn state line shouldn't mean shit to us 'cause we Carolina and we should be as thick as blood"

Tony Rome was speechless, his face a blank mask of uncertainty. He didn't dare try any last minutes heroics because he knew that would be crazy, beyond insane, so he sat meekly before KoKo wondering why the order hadn't yet been issued to terminate him. Maybe Charlotte would spare them.

Looking around, Tony Rome could see that the crib was messed up. Shit was overturned, furniture was busted, blood was everywhere and there were at least three of his people dead or dying. KoKo had really ran up on them with their draws down.

"I don't know how you explain this", KoKo said, "but all I asked for was your support and I was willing to share the loot with you once the war was over, but you wanted to get into some Big Bad Wolf bullshit. And new look at you," KoKo laughed. "You know what? I seriously believe that if I gave you the opportunity you'd do it again. This is war, Tony, and though you Carolina I can't start playing favorites 'cause other motherfuckas will see it as weakness" KoKo turned to his soldiers. "Execute them"

For all practical purposes, the end was near. Early in the morning New York has crossed Princess Anne Road at almost the same spot where they had bum rushed Ingleside during their initial strike, but only this time New York was transported in bullet proof SUV's. This morning they intended to finish Virginia Beach.

Seconds after New York had entered the hood, support vehicles moved in to seal the area off thereby making either escape or evacuation impossible. Everything was set. Virginia Beach would have no choice but to fight to the death or surrender.

"Goddamn!" Lil' Joe shouted, "here the fuck they come!"

"They coming this way?"

"Hell the fuck yeah"

Outside their makeshift Command Center, the Virginia Beach crew could clearly hear the rat-a-tat-tat of rapid machine gun fire as it got closer and closer. And closer.

When Lil' Joe saw the massive armored SUVs, he instantly knew what his options were. He could either get fucked or fight. He made a hurried, frantic phone call to his second-in-command, but when he got no answer, he assumed they had already surrendered. Looking out the window, Lil' Joe saw that New York was too close for him to waste time trying to figure out what had gone down with Q and his posse because he had his own ass to worry about.

"Goddamn!", Lil' Joe cursed again. "It's over"

"Why?" asked Smitty.

"Cause they got our ass cut off and trapped"

"So what we gonna do?"

Lil' Joe had always looked at himself as a true thug soldier, but now for the first time since he had gotten into the game he felt like a bitch. Then he grew defiant. He reached for his gun, holding it, enjoying the feel of its weight in his hand, then without mumbling a word, he ejected the clip and tossed the weapon on the floor. "Put out the white flag"

Justice was not the least bit surprised when he spotted the white flag flapping out of the Virginia Beach Command Center. As a matter of fact, total surrender is what he expected but when he recognized that phase one was over, relief flooded his whole body.

Now that he was in control of Virginia Beach, Justice ordered that Lil' Joe and the others be stripped of their weapons and to await further instructions.

Rah-Rah had to be notified.

Even though Rah-Rah was thoroughly pleased with the absolute success of the mission, he politely refused to interfere in Justice's personal glory, leaving the decision about what to do with the prisoners of war entirely up to his right hand man. As far as he was concerned, Rah-Rah let it be known that he wouldn't lose any sleep over whatever decision Justice made.

Justice, very much aware of how vital his decision would be, decided to study the current crisis in all its ramifications before committing himself to a course of action. He could have Lil' Joe and his people slaughtered or he could spare them but it took only a second before the answer was obvious to him. He would spare the niggas, but Lil' Joe would have to supply troops when New York rolled South. Plus, Lil' Joe would be compelled to pay tribute to New York by giving up a percentage of all the paper made in Virginia Beach until New York got tired of taking it.

As Justice had predicted Lil' Joe was happier than a motherfucka with the decision and on the spot pledged his undying loyalty to New York.

"Your battles are my battles", Lil' Joe announced, "Your enemies. I love who you love"

It was shortly after seven o'clock am when New York left Virginia Beach and it was no exaggeration that Justice was elated with the way New York had performed. And to top it all off, he was delighted that he had resisted the temptation to treat Lil' Joe cruelly. He could have just as easily authorized his execution, but that, more than likely, would have caused a violent protest from his crew who'd have had to be crushed meaning unnecessary bloodshed. Justice knew what a waste of time that would be when there was so much necessary blood to be shed in Charlotte.

KoKo was twisted up. It was like New York had just played another motherfucking trick on him. Niggas was taxing him like he was green and inexperienced, kicking his plans to the curb before he even had the chance to put them into full effect mode. At first, it was that other shit and now here he was again, slamming another one of his combat operations on the inactive list. For one thing, what sense would it make for him to rush to assist VA? None now that they had given up the ghost.

Damn!

KoKo knew he couldn't expect to win if he kept letting Rah-Rah make him put up his toys before he got the chance to play with them. KoKo was dead set on keeping the war contained, to let the whole episode play itself out in VA because win, lose, or draw he didn't want these niggas in Charlotte and it disappointed him that he had failed to stop the advance, but VA had already made their decision. That meant North Carolina was next.

On the one hand, KoKo was bothered by Virginia's quick surrender, but on the other hand he saw it for what it was. It was simply to their advantage. As Richmond and Norfolk had pointed out, they did mad biz'ness with the niggas from up top and didn't lose the financial benefits of getting New York dope.

In all actuality, it may not and was probably not that VA, especially Richmond and Norfolk, was afraid to cross swords with New York. It just don't make good sense financially. As the old saying went, *Why bite the hand that feeds you?* Evidently VA had taken the financial logic of that to heart. Plus, with no more fighting, niggas in VA could concentrate on stacking paper while the rest of the Bottom was still on red alert.

Clearly Rah-Rah knew this well. The nigga probably had experienced a premonition that if VA didn't come under his power as quickly as possible that Charlotte and Memphis would rush in with aid and assistance, presenting a strong united Southern front, but now without VA, both Charlotte and Memphis were back to square one which was to watch their own backs.

That's where Rah-Rah wanted to keep them. Square One.

Chapter 14

Tucked away in a hard to access corridor, conference room number 3 was big and used only for momentous or emergency meetings. And this was both momentous and it was an emergency.

All the men in the room cooled themselves under the whirr of the air conditioner which had been turned up almost to an antic chill, yet most of the men were still sweating though their discomfort had less to do with the temperature then the thought of what might be coming.

Conference room number 3 had never been a welcoming place and though all of the Governors present had all been there before, none of them could boast of ever having had an enchanting moment there. There was no question about that and this time it would be no different.

Or maybe it would.

By the time Tim Rowan from The Department of Justice had finally entered the room, the Governors' hidden terror had surfaced and the big room smelled of fear, but when Rowan, a blond-haired, blue-eyes midwesterner, saw the looks, on their confused faces he laughed jovially

"Gentlemen," he said, "if there is anything that can change the good fortune of this country it is now going on right under your noses"

Rowan was well-known in Washington as a master of political strategy who paid painstaking attention to detail and who usually always pushed all the right buttons. He was also the chief go-to man when one of the government's social experiments had gone off track and someone was needed to fix it. Tim Rowan was Mr. Fix-it.

With his sly, blue eyes twinkling like a pair of diamond-studded stars, he spoke in a big voice, "It has been a long time coming, but even as I speak, niggas are dying in your city streets and you had better not do a damn thing about it"

The men squirmed uncomfortably in their seats, having a difficult time digesting the offered information, but knowing the startling news was highly classified intelligence data which no one would attempt to deny as having come from the top.

"Not long ago, according to all of our most reliable sources, a decades old territorial argument was transformed into an all-out battle for geographical supremacy and as a consequence, Thank God, niggas had finally found an excuse to murder each other indiscriminately, and Washington's unofficial official response is to let the onslaught run its course. Do you understand? Rowan smiled as the men sat silent. "This is a big gift to the government. It's called winning by doing nothing and what could be better? Washington or none of you have to expend any time, talent, or money to negotiate this blessing. We simply let it happen"

"But murder in the streets can hardly be something any right thinking person would endorse"

"Wrong, Governor," Rowan smirked, "and need I mention it again. This is not a developing agenda. It is a directive, meaning none of you can ignore it or act contrary to it in any unforgivable fashion, so you are hereby ordered to notify the respective Mayors as well as their police chiefs and to command them not to disrupt the so called Thug War"

"But----------"

"What your police forces will do as an alternative will be to conduct evacuation procedures to assist in the removal of women and children. Old harmless men also. But no one else", Rowan paused. "Once you leave here, none of you are to have any contact with one another. You are responsible for only what goes on in your own jurisdiction so you must be very sensitive to those issues that affect you personally. This is big, gentlemen, and I'm hoping that none of you jeopardizes his political career with any bleeding heart liberalism. We need the black population thinned out and it's not that we have a cruel streak, but it is a political necessity and this is the best shot we may have at getting a hold on this problem with young, urban males. This is an opportunity not to be missed. Other-wise we may never get this thug problem stepped on"

The Governors, most of them from southern states, sat fixed in place, wondering what to make of this wild development. The government was commanding them to aid and abet murder.

"Don't appear so shocked," Rowan said, "since the rumors have been circulating for a week or more now about a new ORDER coming out of Washington. Well, this is it"

After being offered more details of the directive, the Governors were given a few minutes to confer among themselves before being permitted to ask questions. Sitting in front of them, Rowan pretended to be absorbed in a piece of paper on the top of his briefcase and no one objected when he made a personal phone call, talking loudly and rudely.

When it came time for questions, all of the Governors knew better than to issue any statement of dissent because Washington had already made the final decision for all of them.

Though he experienced regret at having been singled out, the Governor from North Carolina expressed concern that his state might be the site of the bloody war. "And you really think Charlotte--------?"

"From all indicators, it is becoming more and more certain that yes, Charlotte will be the battleground. We have followed the developments as closely as we possibly can, given our distance from the epicenter of the problem. However it does appear that the New York thugs now that they have take full control of Virginia will advance to Charlotte where the major threat lies. At present, we have military personnel following all the movements of the people on both sides and to say the least, they're impressed. The thugs are quite capable of executing precise military operations, all the more reason to wipe them -- well to let them wipe each other out"

"And there is no question that this won't blow over?"

"Not hardly", Rowan grunted. "And hopefully not. I don't want this blowing over, but since it is not a situation we engineered it will require some delicate handling on our part to tie up all the loose ends. It has always been agreed upon that we must devise a system for dealing with the urban male problem in this country and this is what Washington perceives as the perfect solution. Simply let them kill one another. Just think about it, gentlemen. It won't cost us a stinking red cent unlike the prisons which have turned out to be a disaster, rather than being the means to the end we had prayed for. This, however is it, gentlemen, and I'm proud as hell to stand before you and to make this profound announcement"

All the Governors held their breath.

The very next day as the Mayor of Charlotte was preparing to leave his office for the evening, he received a very unexpected visitor who said he had urgent matters to discuss that could not wait or be postponed.

Rowan spoke first after they were seated. "I believe that you should now be apprised of the impending situation Washington has with the so-called Thug War. Am I correct?"

"Yes," Mayor Topper replied. "I spoke personally with the Governor late last evening and if, you're going to check on my response, I submit that I arranged an early morning conference 'with my chief of police ordering him to comply with Washington"

"Good, good" Rowan said, "I'm sure that Washington will applaud your speedy reaction, however I am not here at the behest of the Department of Justice or anyone else in Washington. This visit is strictly personal and I might add highly confidential" Rowan put a finger to his lips to make sure that the Mayor understands that not a word of their conversation was to be repeated.

"I understand and it is an honor that you would pay me a social visit"

Rowan chuckled in amusement. "This is far more than social, Mayor, and though I do not wish to add more tension to an already volatile situation I couldn't bear the hypocrisy a minute more"

"No doubt, I should look to be alarmed by the news you bear then"

"Forewarned and forearmed is more what I had in mind. I'm quite sure your Governor has alarmed you enough"

"Indeed he has. Indeed he has"

Rowan did not particularly look forward to this spur-of-the-moment meeting with a man he had no idea existed until a few hours before he had boarded a flight for Charlotte. The little he had found out about the Mayor during the hours preceding his unannounced visit had been scarcely enough to risk his career for, but he was convinced that Topper could be trusted.

So much had transpired since Washington had gotten wind of the brewing war between Southern and Northern thugs and Rowan knew that the Department of Justice priorities would not change. Washington had long considered it an almost sacred duty to rid itself of The Negro problem which since the Emancipation Proclamation they'd had only marginal success with because any time they had felt they were getting closer to the perfect remedy, there would be a drift in the ambition or passion of the program and the dilemma would be left unresolved.

Full of frustration that nothing had worked to their complete and total satisfaction, Washington seemed happy to toss all its eggs into one basket, throwing its full weight behind 'Get Tough On Crime Legislation' that was designed to rid the inner city of young, urban males. However, the soaring costs of prison construction and yet another drift in policy had threatened to defeat this approach that has worked so well for the last decade. But recognizing no shortsightedness in the plan to stand back and let thugs shoot it out in the inner cities, Washington had eagerly green-lighted the project. Yet there was more and that's what Rowan had come to warn Topper of.

"It is no accident, Mayor, that when it comes to Washington, there is usually more to it than meets the eye and this is due in great measure to Washington's willingness to sacrifice people, places, and things," Rowan shrugged. "Don't ask for examples but I speak with clear-eyed certainty, yet I've never had the courage to make my opinions count. I simply do things or I make sure that things got done. Anyway," Rowan sighed in exasperation, "I'm gonna go out on a limb this time"

"I appreciate that. I think"

Rowan smiled. "Still cautious, huh? Can't say I don't blame you, but here's what's happening. In a nutshell, Washington's secret, hidden agenda is to destroy Charlotte"

"Wh-what?"

"Oh it will be very well-disguised, mind you, but the ruin will be total"

Topper was stunned at the admission. "I-I don't understand how? Why?"

"Rest assured, Mayor, that none of your fabulous skyscrapers will be touched or none of your bridges burned. The damage will be done to your reputation. In other words, Charlotte will be destroyed as the number two banking and financial-hub of America"

Topper slowly nodded, suddenly getting the picture. "I see"

"As you know, New York has always been in a hurry to depose you as second to them. The fear is that Charlotte is too damn good a financial whiz and New York feels that one day you may knock them from their long held perch at number one. New York feels they can better flex their financial muscles without a powerhouse like Charlotte breathing down their necks"

165

"How intriguing," Topper mused. "So, in effect, what will be going on behind the scenes, thanks to you, will be a hidden war, also between New York and Charlotte, to control the country's money"

"Precisely. And to be quite honest, your war with New York is no less serious than the war Charlotte thugs will be waging against New York thugs"

Topper was lost in thought.

"And I must add with no exaggeration that your survival is very closely tied to your city's thugs. They win, you win. They lose........." Rowan let his voice fade, knowing he didn't have to state the inevitable.

"Are you telling me," Topper gasped, "to help out the Charlotte thugs?"

Rowan plopped open a briefcase. "I'm not suggesting anything", he thrust a manila folder into Topper's hand. "Oh, by the way, Kenny Combs is someone you might find interesting. Goes by the name..... KoKo" Topper winked. "Maybe you should buy him a drink one evening"

Topper said nothing, but quickly stuffed the file into his desk.

"And here's someone you already know" Rowan pointed bemusedly at the name on the folder. "Why, that's-that's ----------"

"Of course it is. Your old banking buddy from Atlanta. Well, he wants a piece of your ass. Some friend, that guy"

"Atlanta is teaming up with New York to ruin Charlotte?"

"That would be correct, Mayor. The battle plans are all inside. Mainly Atlanta has been offered enough of the spoils to make them the second largest banking center -------------"

"Goddammit!"

"I understand the sentiment, sir"

The old retired Army general looked at the men crowded around his map. "Now, if I had men under my command and I was positioned here", he pointed. "What I'd do, which would be the only thing to do, would be to deploy my troops about a mile further down the road and set up a defense perimeter from this quadrant rather than where they are stationed now"

"But these are thugs, General, not military strategists"

"Just the same, all of them are shooting real bullets and wanting to get out of this alive"

Terry Shannon, the Governor of New York nodded, looking intently at the map. "But what if Charlotte does decide to bring the battle to Virginia?"

"They won't. So far there has been no sign of movement" The General thought for a moment. "I think that's a sign that they think they are playing it smart by letting Tillman bring the attack to Charlotte. This will put the strain of logistics squarely on New York which by the way will prove to be a formidable operation, could turn into a nightmare. How do you move that many carloads of young, black men down the New Jersey Turnpike without getting at least a couple of vehicles in your convoy picked off? Then there's the question of guns and ammunition"

"Not to mention marijuana" Everyone in the room turned to stare at Arnold Holmes, The black borough President of Harlem. "Weed, a thug never leaves home without the stuff"

"Okay, add drugs to the equation," the General mused. "All of these things combined can spell disaster for New York"

"But they will be getting a free ride"

"Aha, yes, how true, but will the thugs know it? Not in the least so they will not plan as though they are embarking on a Thug Holiday. More than likely to lessen their liability, they will under-pack and how smart do you think it is to run out of bullets in a shoot-out?"

Furious, Shannon picked up an eraser and flung it across the conference room. "Dammit, we're dead even before we get started"

The General stared the Governor down. "The New York thugs are fairly resourceful. After all, they managed to ride into Virginia without mishap and right now they're sitting mighty pretty"

"But what good is that? War is not a business about sitting pretty. It's about killing people and right now I need the thugs in New York to be ambushing the ones in Charlotte", Shannon tried to calm himself. "I don't see why we can't accelerate the hostilities on both sides"

Unnerved, the General took off his glasses. "I don't need your suggestions so why don't you hightail it on back to your duties and let me do the job you're paying me to do"

"There's no bullets flying so how do you explain your paycheck", Shannon's tone was acid.

The General put on his glasses and went back to poring over his map, saying nothing.

"This is not one of your war games, General"

Spinning around, the General shouted. "And neither is it a PlayStation 2 video. In real life you do not move men around with such ease or," he added sarcastically, "such a fitting background soundtrack. Don't worry, you won't lose your bank"

"Then what do you plan to do, General Mobley?"

"I'll get right on it" General Mobley went back to studying his map.

"You better not get sloppy or ----------"

"Goddammit!", the General screamed, giving way to his emotions. "You'll all get what the fuck you want if you'll just leave me alone and let me do my fucking job. I will make sure that Tillman destroys Charlotte. Now will all of you get out of my office. Right now!"

Three hours later, General Mobley got another visitor. Tim Rowan.

"This is more of a gentleman's agreement than anything else, General, but it shall be just as binding as a contract signed under notary"

"I understand"

"It has come to the attention of Washington that you have been paid to see that the New York thugs triumph over their Southern counterparts. Well, you are hereby notified to cease and desist. Leave Mr. Tillman on his own. You are to assist him in no way whatsoever. Understood?"

The General nodded.

"Good"

Rowan left, knowing that if he did this right, he could destroy both New York and Charlotte----------thugs and bankers--------- and in the process transform Washington into the nation's banking Capital.

It was clearly worth a try.

Chapter 15

The trouble began early, but when Killa refused to accept Justice's offer the situation in Memphis almost turned ugly.

Killa was enraged. "We ain't nobody's step-children. What, you New York niggas think we need a big brotha or something, somebody to hold our hand when we cross the goddamn street" That kind of shit didn't delight Killa at all and he was more than willing to let this New York nigga know that he wanted his ass out of town with utmost speed. "Man, you got us fucked up with some other Southern niggas. In Memphis, we choose death over dishonor"

Justice didn't flinch at the temper tantrum. He merely smiled at the kid from Memphis as if Killa was his natural son. "Ain't no need for no drama between us, especially on account of no stupidity on your part, see what I'm saying?" Justice held up his hand to halt another moody outburst from Killa. "Listen, son, what sense does it make to make yourself a target? New York is on the roll and we gonna overthrow the whole South. Whether you like it or not, we coming. We not asking for nobody's permission. We don't look for nobody's approval. We coming"

Upon hearing that Killa calmed down. He had already heard of the slaughter in VA and had already suspected that New York had Memphis in their sight. He also knew that niggas from Richmond, Norfolk and Virginia Beach were down with New York who were probably now poised to swarm the hood and take it over. Killa wouldn't be surprised if niggas from Nashville wouldn't accompany New York on the takedown due to inter-state hatred and beef that had festered for years. Crews from Memphis and Nashville always had their daggers out on each other in the penal system and a lot of time, this long simmering chain-gang animosity journeyed with them to the free world. This alone was damn near enough to convince Killa to embrace the fire (cut a deal) because instinctively he felt that some other New York nigga was breaking bread in Nashville with Knotty Cat, and Killa knew that nigga would not be faithful to the State. Suddenly, Killa did not feel safe.

Justice awaited his order. The two thugs sat in a booth at Tops Bar-B-Q, one of the hottest eating joints in Memphis for over fifty years. Killa bit into his jumbo combo, a massive barbecued pork sandwich.

"Motherfuckas in here do got something beside swine, don't they? If not, I'll have bread and water," Justice chuckled. "Can't fuck with that pig"

"So , y'all finally putting it down like that, huh, New York?"

Justice's face turned serious. "Why sugarcoat it? Yeah, it's like that, Memphis. We coming and we unstoppable" With his voice as cold as steel, Justice spoke calmly. "It is our intention to smash everything that get in our path and our motto is to show no mercy, but the one thing we will do will be to honor our word and stick to any agreements we enter into" Justice stared out from behind his pitch black Oakleys. "And I feel personally that we handling y'all allright by offering you the fig leaf and asking for your friendship and loyalty. Truth be told, son, them niggas in VA would have jumped at the bone", Justice leaned back. "My bad, Memphis. I don't want you to think that New York see y'all like some kind of dogs or nothing, but what I'm saying is that if we would've step to VA with a package like what we handing you, them brothas would have jumped on it with both feet and we wouldn't would have had to unload on 'em, but niggas didn't want to hold hands, so we shook 'em. And it was ruthless", Justice eyed a cutie over the top of his shades. "We can do it again. No doubt"

Meanwhile, Killa's right hand man and others were ready to rep Memphis with blood by picking up their guns and going toe-to-toe with New York because they felt that Memphis belonged to Memphis and should never be somebody else's pussy.

Killa knew how Pimp felt, but Killa didn't believe that the Memphis thugs were accomplished enough or possessed the fighting experience to go into battle with so formidable a foe as New York, so Killa thought that his primary duty was to spare the hood. Still, no matter how good his intentions were, Killa knew that some of his boys if he went to New York would call it paying rent to the niggas up Top.

"But just look at what we're giving you . For one thing, we gonna Big Memphis up, gonna give niggas down here the chance to show and prove. We gonna build a top of the line recording studio so we can put rappers from Memphis in the winner's circle. You saw how tough it was for 8 Ball and MJG. Niggas had skills, but this city lacked the shit needed to promote them. We gonna bring everything, deals, promotions, marketing strategy, that extra push. Everything. Man, give y'all a chance to develop a Memphis style, a Memphis sound.

Save y'all from falling victim to that CRUNK bullshit that's raping the South right about now"

"And the other shit you mentioned?"

"Dawg, you got it"

Killa stuck out his hand. "Deal"

To get all the thugs from Memphis in the back area of the bar at the same time, the pool hall and game room had to be evacuated and closed. As expected, Killa arrived solo without the New York nigga who had disappeared after his meeting with Killa at Tops. Nigga knew he was hated.

When Killa entered the back, Pimp jumped up on a pool table and ordered that everyone shut the fuck up, so everyone could hear every word that had gone down at Tops.

In the back room everyone crowded around except a few niggas who stood in a corner, setting up a video so they could record the whole event and just as soon as the heavy doors closed, the thugs started filming.

Pimp pulled Killa up on the pool table beside him. Niggas cheered loudly.

"Let's give it up for Memphis," Pimp shouted. "This just ain't the Home Of The Blues," he proclaimed. "That's what we do give niggas the Blues"

More mad cheers.

Upon hearing the loud sound of the roaring cheers, Killa, to his own horror, wondered if he had made the right choice. But he had. Memphis' roots were in singing the blues and pimping bitches. Not war.

"Give these niggas the good word, Killa. Tell 'em what it is"

Killa was silent.

"Tell 'em, Killa. When we battle? Tell 'em"

More silence.

"Tell 'em ..... Oh no, Killa, you didn't?", Pimp groaned.

Killa nodded.

"You BITCH!" Pimp shouted as he yanked out a machete and beheaded his best friend. "You bitch motherefucka!"

The hood was a total disaster zone and niggas were out of control. Dead and wounded thugs were laying bleeding on the block as Memphis niggas hunted each other down like beasts.

Pimp, himself, had been beheaded and his lil' brother, J-Love, was castrated. Two other of Pimp's followers were found hanging from the roof of Tops. The niggas on the other side fared no better.

Vicious stabbings and other acts of random violence had been going on in Memphis ever since Pimp had cut Killa's head off two days ago. That gruesome murder, caught on video, had split the city's thug community in half. One side wanting to stand by Killa's deal with New York. The other half favoring war. Now, however, they were at each other's throat.

The angry squall of ambulance sirens split the air, both day and night as thugs ambushed each other without regard for consequences. The hood had gone mad, suddenly changed from whatever it was into a thug burial ground. It was a nightmare where virtually every square inch of the hood was bathed in blood and even after three days the thugs still continued their violent rampage, fascinated by their own mercilessness and there was no end in sight.

When Justice phoned Rah-Rah to keep him abreast of the events in Memphis, Rah-Rah forever the trickster, devised a plan that Justice was to set into motion immediately.

"Make them niggas loot. Trick them country bumpkins into tearing up the white folks' shit"

Justice didn't get it. "What for, Rah? They at each other's throat. Why flip the script? I don't understand"

Rah-Rah weighed the situation carefully. "Because black on black crime don't do nothing for crackers. That's just biz'ness as usual as far as City Hall is concerned, but it's a horse of a different color when niggas start rioting and looting and fucking with shit that don't belong to them. Just think, brer, when the lights went out up here a few years back and niggas started grabbing loot, what the white man do?"

Justice thought for a moment.

"They do the same thing any time niggas get loose and get to ripping off shit from those fancy boutiques and department stores. They impose a goddamn curfew, that's what they white asses do. Put the whole motherfucking hood on lock and don't let 'em move for about three days. You see, son," Rah-Rah chuckled mirthlessly, "if we can get Mr. Charlie to impose a curfew on Memphis for about three days, then we got ourselves a free pass 'cause we won't have to worry about them niggas. They'll be on lock and can't come out to help Charlotte if they wanted to. Nigga come out if his stupid ass want to. Motherfucking National Guard shoot like they snipers" Rah-Rah congratulated himself. "Yeah, son, you get them nigs on lock and we got smooth sailing to Charlotte with no worry about Memphis getting in our shit, see what I'm saying?"

CRUNK

Unknown and unrecognized, Justice and a few of his boys rode past where a large crowd had gathered and shouted out of the car window.

"They looting uptown! Go get all the free shit you want!"

A quick shudder of excitement crackled through the crowd like electricity and without giving it much of a second thought they surged out of the hood. Suddenly bloodshed was out. Looting was in.

Chapter 16

"That cannot be allowed, sir. I'm sorry"

KoKo glared at the pretty woman behind the ticket counter. "Why?"

"Because," the woman replied politely, but curtly, "all Northwest Airlines flights to Memphis have been cancelled"

KoKo offered the same single word again. "Why?"

"Haven't you heard, sir? Memphis is under a 72-hour total curfew"

At that moment, KoKo felt nothing but hate for Rah-Rah because as always the nigga was a step ahead of him, but then his face lit up in a big, wide grin. "Well, Miss, I'd like a round trip ticket to New York City. How about that?"

"No problem, sir. Have a nice flight"

KoKo shrugged. "The flight gonna be a'ight. It's what's gonna happen when I hit the ground that might not be so nice"

"Whatever," the ticket lady said, ready to serve the person in line behind him. Next!"

Rah-Rah moved swiftly. First, in order to take advantage of the situation in Memphis, he put a squad of New York thugs on the road into Tennessee. They would bang into Carolina from the east. Then another squad, the VA posse would storm them from the North and when Charlotte had been softened up enough, he would bum rush them from the bottom via the ATL.

On the morning that he sent out his death squads, he had conferred briefly with his captains.

"Do this damn thing quickly," he commanded. "No mercy. No surrender. No retreat"

Once KoKo had gotten put up in his hotel suite in Manhattan, he felt compelled to contact Coot down in North Carolina to let him know which direction shit was going in, but mainly he wanted to find out where Coot's heart was. Motherfuckas was switching grooves and flipping the script like it was a part on the game plan KoKo didn't need any last minute surprises, especially not from North Carolina.

KoKo considered how much he trusted Coot and in some measure it stressed him when he found that his trust was not absolute. Thugs were not the most predictable people in the world and given their appetite for the double cross, KoKo was left to ponder how much it would take for Coot to commit the crime of thug treachery and to go over to the other side.

"We're the last ones left," KoKo admitted. "It's us by our lonesome. Memphis dead and niggas can't be revived"

"That's where you at?"

"Naw, but trust me they all in"

"New York coming then?"

KoKo admitted quite frankly they were. "We ready, though, on my end. Y'all on strapdown up there?"

"Ain't no question. How else we gonna command the respect of them niggas?"

KoKo confessed to that truth. "Sho' you right, homeboy, but them niggars sending motherfuckas to hell so I can't help but feel--------"

"Don't sweat it, KoKo 'cause I can't think of nothing them niggas can do to us that we can't do to them"

"Niggas from them other hoods probably said the same shit and look what happened to they asses. Same shit can happen to us if we start faking and let them slip in on us before we can get our shit tight"

"Why you tripping, dawg?"

KoKo was amazed that Coot would ask him that, but it didn't matter. "We gotta meet them niggas with overwhelming power"

"We got it, dawg. It's all good"

"Will you die for the thug nation of the South, Coot? Are you 100% willing to give your life in the cause?"

Coot's tone grew sterner, more confident. "I am a thug and I believe in the South and hell yeah I will fight to the death. I am ready to die, KoKo, but even better than that, I am ready to kill any motherfucka that thinks he can come on our stomping ground and make us bow down. Better dead than a goddamn coward. Bet that, my nigga 'cause just as sho' as my word is bond, that's good money"

"Then I'm making you the general of all the soldiers from Carolina. Unite them, Coot, because if we can't master ourselves then how can we defeat the enemy? I will be gone for a few days and everything is in your hands until I get back. I hate to put this kind of pressure on you, but you can't sleep on them niggas. They got us squeezed in on three sides, from Virginia up top, from Tennessee to our west, Atlanta at our ass. And, the Atlantic Ocean cutting us off from the east", KoKo sighed, "I'm counting on you Coot"

"As I done proved over and over again in my life", Coot said with boast, "I am a thug nigga worthy of trust"

"Thanks, Coot"

"Just do what you gotta do. Do you. I got this little bit"

"I don't know how much time you got ----------"

"Man, I wouldn't give a damn if the motherfuckas was outside right now knocking on my goddamn door, I'll fight they ass off with a butter knife and a fly-swatter"

KoKo trusted Coot absolutely.

Coot was swollen with pride. He was thrilled that KoKo had given him command of all the NC thugs because this was quite an honor, one that he would turn into triumph. He was determined to show and prove that KoKo had made the right choice. This was a larger than life opportunity and though he had not yet got around to revealing his full offensive, he had made up his mind not to concentrate the battle in Charlotte.

That would be his first order of biz'ness. To tear all the NC thugs' focus away from Charlotte as the primary battle site though everybody was salivating to fight there. What he now planned do was to fight the up North crew in the middle of the State which would provide him with a much needed center of defense. He liked that idea much better than the one based on Charlotte because the Queen City has its ass sitting right on the South Carolina line which made it much more vulnerable to attack from Atlanta. Also his center-of-the-State plan would make it harder for them to get clamped down on from Tennessee.

Plus by forcing the invading posse to roll farther into the State would make it a helluva lot easier for North Carolina to surround them, cut off their supply lines and succeeding at this would permit the down home thugs to slam into the niggas Yankees, snapping the whip on their asses until the motherfuckas either surrendered or got done.

Coot would also take the liberty of further insulating his thug troopers by boosting their striking capacity by accelerating the movement of his backup thugs from the little, small towns along the corridor of the 12th District.

His strategy, as simple as it appeared in theory, would require a highly effective communication system as well as the energy to move lighting quick. Coot knew, understood, and accepted the risks. Still, no major drawbacks came to mind and already the roar of victory pounded in his head. And that was all it took to convince him that he could punish New York and have them niggas yoked and chained even before they had the damn chance to put their fingers on the triggers of their biscuits.

Coot mentally went back over the checklist of shit he had to do with the quickness and after a rapid review of the basic stuff, he discovered he was ready to bring the noise. If shit was going to go wrong, Coot surmised that it would be at the mouth of the 12th which would be a stress point since the border of the State would have to be defended fiercely. The first encounter would be critical for both sides, North and South, so Coot knew his command of the situation there had to be precise and error free.

183

Coot almost decided to take the first four hour shift on the border to observe and intercept traffic on 1-85, but he swiftly corrected that oversight. He'd send in thugs from Apex and some of the smaller towns instead, giving his main force from Raleigh/Durham the chance to stabilize any unattended biz'ness they might have on the block because once the gunsmoke kicked off, the paper-getting would have to cease. It would then be time to kill.

Coot issued his orders.

And then all hell broke loose!

Iron Mike sensed it before his mind had time to respond. It was New York! Making full use of the element of surprise, the Puerto Ricans gave combat to the NC border thugs, pounding them with steady gunfire, pushing them out of position, disrupting their reflexive instincts, all of which combined to make the Southern thugs sitting ducks.

Surprised that he could not isolate the Latino thugs or put together a big enough counteroffensive to impede their forward momentum, Iron Mike screamed into his cell phone for backup.

Firing away over the hood of his ride, Iron Mike cursed himself for getting played. Somehow the image of truckloads of Latinos, dressed as migrant farm workers, had failed to trigger alarm in his head. Shit, he had thought they were Mexicans. Now he was paying dearly for that mistake.

After the first wave of the attack was over, Iron Mike calculated that he had lost 80% of his posse, but he prevailed upon the remnants of his soldiers to keep on blazing away.

Within another 30 seconds, Iron Mike began to regret that he hadn't had sense enough to order a retreat. Now it was too late. Another two truckloads of New Yorkers barreled in and bore down on them from a 45 degree angle, coming in hard.

Despite the fact the they were pinned down, Iron Mike and his boys fought back desperately and though the momentum of the battle never turned in their favor, Iron Mike realized he could maintain his position if he could somehow collapse the center of the second wave of attackers. Much of the damage, NC had been able to inflict upon New York was done by Big Hank who was putting in mad work with the street sweeper. He was sprawling some asses out, but when Big Hank went to work on the second crew of Puerto Ricans, they were already in retreat, their mission accomplished. Iron Mike saw what had happened and gazed in wild-eyed awe as Justice and the real New York thugs freely thundered down the Interstate covered by the firepower of their Latino counterparts.

New York was in the house!

And that he concluded was the last thing KoKo would have wanted, but it wasn't like he had invited the motherfuckas in. Niggas had G-Thanged their way in and as Iron Mike watched New York breach NC's security zone, he presumed that the calm and quiet of the State was about to get louded up with the rat-a-tat-tat of automatic weapons because New York's only interest was in disturbing the peace.

Aside from taking a brief second to shed a tear for all the dead motherfuckas from the same side of the tracks as him, Iron Mike knew he had no time to waste. He had to regroup, to extend the battle until all the thugs from Carolina met.

When Iron Mike called Coot, he wished his phone had a camera on it so he could send Coot a photo of the dead bodies strewn across the highway so he could get a clearer picture of what they were up against. Motherfuckas were representing, acting like thugs from New York defined the true essence of what "putting in work" meant.

Iron Mike tried not to sound discouraged when he passed on his report, but it was extremely difficult to keep his emotions controlled.

"Motherfuckas fool, Coot. They on something"

Even with the little info he had available, Coot sensed that NC could go limp if the niggas from up top weren't given serious combat soon, but Coot decided that the best course of action for the time being was to stop the small border skirmishes since they would only exhaust his thugs' resistance. Coot realized that it was now or never so he gave the final order, to prepare to fight to the last man.

The Great Thug War was going to go down in, of all places, a vineyard. Little known or talked about was North Carolina's wine-producing region, a lush landscape of wineries nestled in the Yadkin River Valley at the foot of the Blue Ridge Mountains.

Access to the region was usually tightly monitored, but since this was very early in the wine-growing season the grapeyards would be practically empty, the perfect battlefield. Of the 33 vineyards in the area, Coot had picked the one at Westbend, the oldest, as best suited for Thug Armaggedon.

If New York would agree to the site, they could enter the valley from Winston-Salem, leaving the NC thugs to come in from the opposite end of the region. The vineyards were easily accessible from the Interstate and since there were a good number of bed-and-breakfast Inns in the Yadkin River Valley both groups would have ample lodging while they made their battle plans.

This was a war between thugs and Coot saw no reason to jeopardize the lives and property of square niggas. He was well aware, though, of New York's desire to sack Charlotte, an intention they had made clear early. New York felt that Charlotte was the heart of the thug nation in the Carolinas and that by defeating Charlotte convincingly, they could dismantle all the hoods in the State and put down New York law. That was one reason. The other was that New York wanted to make Charlotte thugs leak as retaliation and revenge for the murder/mutilation of Bone, Kool G., Red Devil, and Robot, who had met their Maker in Charlotte. And, for this New York vehemently despised the Queen City. Still, if the war was being waged to determine once and for all what thugs would be left standing, then the battle site should be either secondary or irrelevant.

Coot felt that in the vineyard, the war wouldn't have to be strictly controlled since there would be no children or cars to get in the way. Out here in the wide, open spaces they could shoot it out like the crackers did in their Civil War. Niggas could handle their biz'ness in the same way. Go down in Thug History.

Coot sighed in resignation. If only one thing was certain it was that win, lose, or draw this battle would make history. He hoped New York would get down like that, show that thugs could be gentlemen also. If so, it was getting ready to go down!

KoKo had pride. He was ready to fight the New York niggas wherever they showed up, in the streets, in the parks, on the highways, at church. Anywhere and everywhere, but he did like Coot's idea to contain the war, to dress the conflict in the formal garb of the first Civil War where soldiers fought, fell back, regrouped, charged again, over and over, until one side or the other had had enough and surrendered.

After shooting Rah-Rah an e-mail, KoKo waited for a response and got a telephone number.

"Sorry, country-assed nigga," Rah-Rah growled, "but we ain't down there on no old timey shit like that. I know y'all

187

niggas slow, but damn I didn't know y'all was that far behind the times"

"I thought y'all niggas supposed to be real warriors?"

"We are and that's why we gonna take it to y'all punk asses wherever we find you. We'll fight you in the trenches or on the rooftops, but it ain't gonna be no video game war, nigga. We pushing on to Charlotte"

"But what if we ain't there when you get there?"

"Then this is how it will go down, country boy. We'll give you 24 hours to come out and fight"

"And if we don't?"

"Then we start raping all the women and putting one in the head of all the young niggas. No bullshit, son. I'll see you in Charlotte or else. I'm out.

KoKo hung up. He had to launch Plan B. This was life during wartime.

Chapter 17

Even from a distance, Rah-Rah's estate in Westchester County looked awesome and it appeared much more impressive in the daylight than it had last night when KoKo had rolled through, checking out the landscape.

Scoping it out from where he was he gave KoKo a spectacular view of the ground layout, but just as Shine had told him a while back, the mansion had an amazing security system. And then there were the dogs.

KoKo lowered the binoculars and gently rubbed his eyes, but he quickly raised them again. There was activity at the mansion. A black Mercedes pulled around to the front of the expensive crib and parked as a beautiful, young lady jumped out and dashed to the front door. Evidently, her passenger was late.

The woman dressed casually, entered the home and a short while later emerged with a young boy -------Rah 3-------in tow.

School –time!

KoKo studied the pair for a scant second longer then lowered the binoculars. He quickly eased behind the wheel of his rental car and sped down the empty stretch of road to a spot perhaps 100 yards away where the Mercedes would have to pass to connect with the main traffic artery leading back to Manhattan.

KoKo was not concerned about getting made by the woman because it was the time of morning when there was a lot of traffic leaving Westchester heading into New York, but still he drove cautiously. He slipped a Lil' Jon CD into the dash and the Crunk boomed out of the car's system and flowed smoothly into his veins like a bonafide drug. After that he and the music were one. He was Crunk! To death!

At precisely 8:00 am, the black Mercedes rolled to a complete halt in front of an exclusive private school. A second car pulled up, unloading a student. KoKo pulled up pretending that he too had a passenger to deliver, but when he saw Rah 3 leave the Mercedes he was so amped that he could damn near hear the boy's footsteps as he strolled off.

Flushed with adrenaline, KoKo waited impatiently as the black Mercedes pulled off and then exited his car in a heated rush, tracking Rah 3 like a hungry lion. When he got to where Rah 3 stood, KoKo realized that he didn't look as much like a teacher as he would have preferred, but it was far too late for any second guesses now. This was a GO.

KoKo looked around, his eyes going every which way at once, scanning the huge throng of students who milled about bullshitting as they awaited the school bell to ring, signaling the start of class. Getting close, KoKo altered his angle of approach. He wanted to bypass the three white girls. Bitches get a whiff of what was going down and would no doubt panic, bursting out in a chorus of shrieks and yells, sure to draw attention to him. And he didn't want to make that mistake. Presumably Rah 3 had been schooled in how to conduct himself in the event of a hostage situation. At least that's what Shine had told him. Therefore he wasn't overly concerned about Rah 3 trying to shout or scream as he knew this would only endanger his life more.

KoKo glanced over his shoulder at the three girls who were busy chewing bubble gum and talking excitedly. He drifted into the unoccupied space next to the cute boy.

"Raymond Tillman?"

"Yes sir", Rah 3 eyes were unquesting.

"I am a friend of your father"

Rah 3 flinched, his eyes now wide question marks as if he instinctively understood what that lie meant. "I know all of my father's friends" Rah 3 stood tall, looking brave, staring up at KoKo. "If you were a friend I would know you"

KoKo stooped down, a reflex action, and stared into the boy's eyes. "You know what's happening, don't you, Rah 3?"

"So you're not a friend of my daddy?"

KoKo grabbed the kid's hand, the movement swift but gentle. "I am not going to hurt you, but I do need you to come with me, okay?" KoKo took possession of Rah 3's book bag. "Your daddy did tell you how to act if you ever", KoKo couldn't finish the sentence. "You're not going to scream or try to run, are you?"

"No, but I do need to call my daddy so I can let him know how much money you want"

"You can call in a little while, "KoKo mumbled softly, "But right now I want you to walk with me to my car. I promise you I will not harm you" He patted the boy's head. "I give you my word on that"

Walking casually toward the dark blue car, every few steps KoKo would lean his head down and whisper words of reassurance to Rah 3 who moved carefully in step, knowing precisely what was expected of him.

"When will I get the chance to call my daddy?"

"Soon, real soon, but when you talk to him you're going to have to pay close attention to what I tell you to say to him, okay?"

Rah 3 nodded. "I know"

KoKo felt a sudden sadness for the boy, but remembered that this was war times and that certain unpleasantries had to be performed. There was just no getting around that fact. Still. KoKo didn't like doing what he was doing. "If you just keep in mind that I'm not going to let anyone hurt you, I think this situation will go a lot easier for you"

"Okay" Rah 3 responded, resigned to his fate, thinking that this was merely a stunt for money which his father would readily pay, no matter the amount, to secure his release. That explained Rah 3 total lack of terror at the whole ordeal. He had probably been groomed for an event like this since he had been old enough for school.

At the car, no one appeared particularly distressed that the Tillman boy was leaving school with a strange man. No one, in fact, even seemed to have noticed.

Just as KoKo drove off, the school bell sounded, shattering the morning's calm and all the students scampered to class. Rah 3's eyes were uninterested. He looked away and gazed straight through the front window.

"What we're going to do today," KoKo commented in a kid friendly tone, "is going to be much more exciting than school. As a matter of fact, when we get where we're going, I got somebody I want you to meet. Know what her name is?"

Rah 3 shook his head.

"Her name is Janeen"

Thanks, in larger part, to Rah 3's home training the kidnapping had come off much smoother than anticipated and it seemed to KoKo that finally he was in control. Still he would proceed with caution. Extreme caution.

All the way to Connecticut, KoKo had closely observed Rah 3's reactions and although the kid had remained emotionless and uncommunicative, KoKo noticed that the boy was quietly absorbing everything he saw, getting all the details. Rah 3 had been taught well.

It had taken the Governor of North Carolina two days to get a contact number for Kenny Combs, the one attached to his personal cell phone. It had been assigned to his common-law wife, Kendra, but this still didn't explain why he wasn't answering.

It would have been much easier to have issued a Governor's Warrant for his arrest, but he preferred to pursue this as a low-level security concern to insure there would be no civilian panic until he had figured out how to defuse the situation. Additionally, he didn't want to do anything to jeopardize any war plans Mr. Combs had which may have qualified as strategy against the northern thugs. The Governor, in his heart, prayed that Mr. Combs had a war strategy. Failing that, they both would be sunk.

The second problem the Governor had beside Mr. Combs not answering his phone was that time was running out because, whatever the man was doing to maintain his communications was sure as hell not based on telephone contact.

"Mayor," the Governor growled, "get over to the Combs' residence and do whatever you must to get his mother to call him on his cell phone. Here's the number"

"Haven't you tried it?"

"Hell yeah, I've tried. He won't answer. Probably will need a code or something or else he only responds to numbers on that phone that he recognizes. I'm quite sure that if his mother's number popped up, he'd answer, so get to it, Mayor"

"You're not going to do anything to interfere-------"

"Just keep your eyes open, Mayor, and your damned mouth closed and do as you're instructed"

"What is it you suggest?"

"Just what I've already told you. Get your ass over to the Combs' residence and tell his mother that we need to speak with her son. You don't have to explain the nature of the emergency, but do let her know it is a crisis"

"Should I then have the young man contact you?"

"With all deliberate speed, I might add"

Rah-Rah felt great this morning. Soon the entire thug nation would be under one king, him. He would one day be the voice of thugs far and wide. The South was merely the beginning and he would not cease his quest until every thug in the country bowed down to him. Now that victory in the south was a done deal, Rah-Rah pondered the alliances he would make and those whom he would crush. What he, first of all, would do, would be to establish a strong central government, most likely in Charlotte, where he could consolidate his power and usher in a period of relative calm and prosperity. Then he would strengthen his army and extend peace offerings to the Midwest and West, sending out emissaries to bring them into the newly established empire on which the sun would never set. Jersey, Philly, and DC would however get nothing but grief from him. Rah-Rah was quick to acknowledge that.

Motherfuckas ain't had nothing coming, not after the attitude they had bought him when he called upon them for assistance.

Rah-Rah laughed. While he planned his future he also plotted those niggas funerals, but that's how shit in the game went. No big deal.

As the true king of the Thug Nation, Rah-Rah would treat everyone who paid homage to him as he would his son, but woe to the hood who disobeyed him and no motherfucka had better think twice about withdrawing from the nation because the consequences of that were too severe even for him to contemplate.

And so it was while Rah-Rah was in this expansive frame of mind that his cellphone rang. Immediately he felt uneasy as a suffocating sense of dread crawled all over his body. This was his RingMaster dial tone and it was to be used only in case of an emergency. A cold chill frosted Rah-Rah's spine because the only two people who could access him via RingMaster was his women and his son. Rah-Rah grew weak in the knees. His woman was in the den, so that could only mean one thing.

He snatched open the phone.

"Rah 3?"

"Daddy, this man got me-------"

"Put the motherfucka on, Rah 3" Rah-Rah almost shouted. "Give him the phone. Everything is going to be alright, son, so don't worry, okay? You'll be home soon. Now, put that man on"

"So how do we solve this problem, nigga? And in case you need to know, this is Charlotte"

"If you do anything to harm a hair-------"

"Your son is fine and it's a simple matter for him to remain like that or we could play blow-for-blow, nigga" KoKo's voice grew ice cold. "What if I gave you the ultimatum to either submit or get your Lil' boy Nick Berged. If you haven't had the chance to view the video of what the Iraqis did to Nick Berg, I urge you to -------"

"You motherfucka! You a bitch if you gotta use a harmless child as a pawn"

"This is war, enemy of mine, and all is fair. I took it like a trooper when you put down my boys"

"But they were soldiers"

KoKo laughed evilly. "Sometimes sons must suffer for the sins of their father. Wrath don't discriminate, nigga"

"What do you want? For me to spare Charlotte?"

"Hell naw, motherfucka, Charlotte don't need no goddamn sparing"

"You want us to hook up, then?"

KoKo laughed. "That would be disrespecting the memory of my troopers 'cause that was why you executed them. 'Cause I wouldn't bow down or hook up wit' your ass"

"Then what do you want in exchange for my son? Call it"

"To be specific-------nigga, hold on. Let me deal with this other call and I'll holla right back at your ass, fool"

"Don't put me on hold, motherfucka," Rah-Rah shouted. "Don't be playing no fucked up games with my son's life, nigga I-------"

"Hold on, ho" KoKo clicked over. "Ma?"

"Boy, what you done now? I got the Mayor at my house"

"The Mayor?"

"Said he needs to talk to you. Say it's important and he right here now, waiting. Here he is"

"Mr. Combs, this is as your mother has informed you, Mayor Anderson, and what we must speak to you about is a matter of extreme emergency"

"We ?"

"The Governor and I"

"The Governor?! Put my moms back on for a minute"

"Hello"

"Ma, you sure that's the Mayor and not-------"

"Boy, I know the Mayor when I see him and this is the Mayor, the same, exact one I voted for"

"Ma," KoKo pleaded, "you sure?"

"Kenny, it's the Mayor. What, you think your own Mama don't know one white man from another when she sees one?"

"Okay, Ma, put him back on"

"As I was saying, Mr. Combs, this is an issue of State security and I'm sure you have plenty of questions, many of which I'm probably totally unqualified to answer, but-------"

"Then why you bothering me if you unqualified to answer my question?"

"I'm clicking you over to the Governor, Mr. Combs. Hold on, please"

To judge by what he had heard so far KoKo couldn't make heads or tails out of what was going on and he didn't want to ruin his chances of getting some answers by jumping the gun on the Governor. He still knew he had Rah-Rah on the other end, but he didn't figure the nigga was going anywhere. Apparently he had Rah-Rah's undivided attention which is what he wanted, but evidently he had also flown into the radar of some heavy duty politicians. At a minimum, he did halfway know what to expect out of Rah-Rah while with the Mayor and the Governor he was positively clueless. Still he could not afford to allow himself to dwell on shit over which he had no control.

"Governor" The Mayor rasped. "He's on the line now"

"Mr. Combs, this is the Governor"

"I know that much," KoKo said brusquely, "but what do you want, that's the question?"

"We have ourselves a dilemma, Mr. Combs"

"Involving who-------the police?"

The Governor took a short breath. "Rest assured, Mr. Combs, that you have nothing to fear from the law enforcement community. You have my assurances of that"

As far as he could presently tell, KoKo had no deliberate reason to doubt the Governor's attempt to relieve him of doubt, but without so much as a single clue as to what was actually happening, it was impossible for him to properly assess and evaluate the situation or to make the correct choice, provided he was given one. He would have to play it by ear.

"What is this about, Mr. Governor?"

"You've been lucky so far, Mr. Combs"

"Lucky?" KoKo quizzed. "How?"

"I'm making direct references to the Thug War"

Even though there was no mistake about what he'd heard, KoKo still couldn't believe he had heard it, not coming from, of all people, the Governor, and not in so casual a tone.

"Mr. Tillman, Rah-Rah to you, is a shrewd son-of-a-bitch. He's done practically everything that he has needed to do to become a real threat to you, to Charlotte"

KoKo sat in stunned silence, not knowing how or even if he should respond.

"If the truth must be known, Mr. Combs, you don't stand much of a chance, will have what little chance you have reduced even more if Mr. Tillman conducts a simultaneous breakout from the perimeters of his three major arteries of attack. I hate to say this, Mr. Combs, but due to your poor combat judgment, you won't come out of this alive. New York will either massacre you with superior gunfire or chase you into the Atlantic Ocean to drown like rats," the Governor paused dramatically. "I can help"

"I don't know about no Thug War"

"Listen, Mr. Combs, we don't have the time to play games. Let's be clear on that. Let's also be clear that my promise of assistance is no empty gesture. I have as much to lose as you, if not more, so therefore our fates are tied together in this Thug War. That being true, we would be far better off if we pitched in together to clean this mess up"

"Let's hear more"

"What more do you need to hear, for Christ's sake, Mr. Combs? What on God's green earth do you think you have that can slow Mr. Tillman down?"

"His little boy," KoKo blurted without thinking. "I have his son"

"Even that may not be enough," the Governor muttered icily, "but given the fucking hole you've dug for yourself I can imagine why you would think so"

KoKo cast a dirty look at the phone. Who did this motherfucka think he was?

"Go to Manhattan"

"H-How do you know where I am?"

"Global positioning. We run the coordinates off your phone signals. Relax, I don't intend to give your position away because like I said, Mr. Combs, we're brother-in-arms in this way"

"Go to Manhattan and do what?"

I have a trusted confidant there. I want you to meet with him. He'll advise you and tell you best how to use Mr. Tillman's son to you're our advantage. Now, get going, Mr. Combs.

KoKo clicked back over to Rah-Rah. "Unfortunately, nigga, something just came up. I'll holla back at you later"

"Man look-------"

"Your son is safe. You got my word on that"

199

"Well, when I'm gonna hear from you again?"

"In, let say, four hours"

"Why so goddamn long?"

"Cause I said so, nigga, that's why"

KoKo hung up.

"Who the fuck is this?", Rah-Rah yelled into the receiver, "And, how did you get this number?"

"None of that is important, Mr. Tillman, but what I have to say is, so please listen carefully. I am Governor Rand-------"

"Governor Rand?! Of New York?!"

"At your service, Mr. Tillman"

"Is this some king of joke?"

"Do you hear me laughing, Mr. Tillman. In fact, the matter we, you and I, need to discuss is probably the most vital conversation you'll ever have in your life and on that note, I'm telling you that it is in your best interests, as well as mine------- to assign this as top priority"

"I don't even know what this is about," Rah-Rah said warily.

"I'll explain, but not over the phone"

Rah-Rah was immediately suspicious. This could be another one of Charlotte's trick. Already they had managed to snatch his son and maybe now this was a ploy to grab him, so at this point he felt that meeting with someone even if the motherfucka said he was the goddamn Governor was very ill-advised.

"I don't meet with strangers"

The Governor laughed grimly. "God knows, you've probably done worse things than that in your life, but I can understand your reluctance. Charlotte is such a thorn in the side, wouldn't you agree, Mr. Tillman?"

Rah-Rah was suddenly on full alert. "What about Charlotte? You with them?"

"I am who I say I am" The Governor sighed, exhaling through his nose.

"But how do I know that?"

"You don't, hold on a second. Do you happen to be in possession of one of those camera phones. I would think a man of your..."

"Yeah, I have one"

"Great. Well, it's only great if you know what the Governor of New York look like. Do you, Mr. Tillman, know what I look like?"

"Send the flick. I know what the Governor looks like" When Rah-Rah received the phone, he stared at it for a couple of quick seconds and was instantly convinced that the caller was legit. He was the goddamned Governor. "Yeah, It's you"

"Thanks," the Governor said. "It's nice to be recognized, but now that the phone shoot is over, we need to discuss some top secret strategy concerning a common problem of ours"

"Charlotte? I don't get it"

"In time, everything will be explained, but first------"

"They kid------" Rah-Rah voice stopped.

"Mr. Tillman? Are you still there, Mr. Tillman?"

"Yeah" Rah-Rah decided not to go bitching to the white man about his son.

"You can win this Thug War, Mr. Tillman, if you do exactly like I tell you. Not only that------Mr. Tillman, are you still there?"

"I'm here"

"What, you didn't think I knew about the Civil War between The North and The South. I know, Mr. Tillman, and I'm prepared to do everything in my power to make sure you beat the hell out of the South. What do you think, Mr. Tillman?"

"With all due respect sir, but I don't know what the hell you're talking about"

"And with even greater due respect, Mr. Tillman, I say you're full of shit"

"I'm sorry that you made a mistake, Governor"

"Well, I find it interesting that you're going to tell me that you know virtually nothing of blowing shit off the map in Virginia Beach, or about a little trip down I-85 with a truckload of Latinos. What about Memphis? I don't even have the heart to tell you the truth about your friends Bone, Kool G., and the others, and since I'm afraid that I've either lost you or made, as you say, a mistake, I won't even mention what else Charlotte has in store for your dumb ass. The only mistake I may have made, Mr. Tillman, is that I had led myself to believe you were much smarter than you've proven to be so far this morning"

Rah-Rah took a deep breath. "How do I know this is not a trap?"

"Because, goddammit, Mr. Tillman, I need you. Look, we must act quickly if we're going to handle this assignment, but I need to know if you're game for my assistance"

Rah-Rah remained quiet.

"May I presume that your silence signifies consent?"

Rah-Rah said nothing.

"Good. I'll tell you where to meet my people. I'll call again shortly. Relax, Mr. Tillman, you just won the war"

Rah-Rah felt he was going to win anyway, but maybe the Governor could help get Rah 3 back sooner. It was worth a try.

It took just over five minutes for the Governor of New York and Charlotte to get in touch with each other and since they had agreed to cooperate with one another and not to interfere directly in the Thug War, their conversation was brief.

"I guess I should let you know that my boy has your boy's kid, holding him as a pawn" The Governor of North Carolina smiled. "Check"

"But not checkmate"

"Mr. Tillman didn't mention it to you?"

"No. The bastard didn't mention it"

"Probably too fucking embarrassed. Anyway, the kidnapping was a smart move on Charlotte's part, levels the playing field a bit"

"Not by much, though. My boy had your boy dead in the water, was getting ready to squeeze-------"

"Bullshit. In just a few days North Carolina was prepared to launch a counterstrike that would have had you Yankees running for you lives"

The New York Governor laughed loudly. "You wish. Too bad this won't go down on record"

"Why?"

"Because it would be another win for the North. By the way what was your boy intending to ransom the kid for?"

"Never said. What difference does it make?"

"None. Just curious"

"Oh by the way, if New York wasn't such 'fraidy cats, they would meet North Carolina in the valley"

"What fucking valley?"

After Governor Monroe of North Carolina had explained, Governor Rand started muttering something about the final solution.

"But we already have the final solution" Governor Monroe frowned.

"But not the ultimate, final solution"

"And you do?"

"I do"

"Let's hear it, Governor"

"Simple. You say New York refuses to fight in that grape patch down there?"

"Cowards"

"That can be fixed"

"How?"

"Tell your Mr. Combs to ransom Tillman's son for the opportunity for the two thug armies to meet in battle at your godforsaken grape patch. To get his boy back safe, Tillman will give his thugs their marching papers"

"That's a very kindly offer"

"I think so"

"Then we just let 'em go at it?"

"Not quite"

"What do you mean, not quite. I've got a damn lot riding on this"

"As if I don't"

"So what do you suggest?"

"A compromise of sorts where we both win one for the overall good of the country. I think that's a better objective than which state has the biggest goddamned banks"

"Funny you should say that"

"And what's even funnier is that my position wouldn't change if our respective positions were reversed. America

204

CRUNK

needs this a helluva lot more than either New York or Charlotte"

"What's your plan or should I say what's your scheme?'

Governor Rand clapped his hands merrily. "I like scheme a lot better, makes everything a bit more devious, wouldn't you agree, Governor?"

"I wouldn't know much about that. We don't have as much of a taste for scandal as you Northerns. No offense, but we're slow Joe when it comes to cheating, manipulating, and scheming"

"Well, dammit, I'm proud to say I'm no slouch in that area, so you just get your boy to make the offer and I'll get mine to accept it"

"And then what?"

Governor Rand chuckled. "And then the thug world will be one step closer to total extinction and I think every decent American citizen, white or black, can learn to live with that"

"I'm in, Governor. Let's do it"

"God save the Queen"

"We don't have a Queen, Rand"

"Soon, that's what everyone will be saying about thugs"

"What?"

"We don't have any!"

The Governors laughed.

Chapter 18

Governor Rand didn't expect to have to tussle too hard to get his way with the military personnel and he didn't. He got his operational plans fully approved with only a minimal amount of resistance and this related to man hours required to complete the assigned mission.

"I want the entire installation blanketed and I want to be able to follow everything by satellite"

"Just out of curiosity," one of the military men asked, "why pictures?"

"This doesn't happen often"

"But this could cause a great deal of embarrassment----"

Governor Rand scowled. "These are criminal thugs, people who need to be disposed of, so just do your job. As you know, I have the permission of the President and he expects this to conform to specifications"

"We'll know soon enough," the military man grunted. "That's for damned sure"

KoKo regretted that he couldn't see the expression on Rah-Rah's face, but he was sure it was screwed up into a mask of anger.

"So, like I was saying, nigga, that's what your bitch ass gotta do to get your kid back. Meet me on the killing floor"

Rah-Rah nodded to himself. "You got that, dawg. That'll work. When will I get my son back?" Even though originally he had sincerely desired to fight in Charlotte, Rah-Rah discovered he had no major issues or complaints about battling in the vineyard, especially now that he didn't have any other choice. Now more than ever he wanted to destroy Charlotte.

"Your son will be returned when you move your boys in"

"This evening, then"

"Cool"

Both thugs were relatively surprised at the calm at which they handled the final war negotiations. They discussed the matter as if they were comparing notes on who had the flyest rims when instead they were making plans for the most intense blood-shedding in this country since the 1860s. Both Rah-Rah and KoKo knew the tally of the dead would be extremely high, but they didn't talk about that. They both also knew that it would signal the end for one as a force in the thug world, but that was something else they didn't mention. Instead, they focused on everything that would take place before the actual start of the battle because neither was willing to divulge anything that might alert the other to their strategy.

"Is there anything else we need to discuss?"

"And this will be your first time at the spot?"

"Yeah, nigga, so don't start no shit like we got some kind of homecourt advantage. This is neutral territory"

"I just don't want y'all country niggas trying to pull no tricks"

"In the South, we give a man a fair fight so finally you 'bout to get what you been begging for a goddamn killing. Man, I ain't gonna feel no sympathy for you 'cause you brought it to us"

"We brought it, son, 'cause we can handle it"

"Then all talk dead. You move your boys in and I'll do the same. Saturday is a free day. Both sides can move about and study the layout of the killing floor and set up defense posts and battle stations"

"That's a bet, son"

"Then Sunday at daybreak"

"Bet that, son. Bet that"

KoKo exhaled deeply. "Why you brought this upon yourself, I guess I'll never know, but you're gonna regret it, I guarantee you that"

"When will I get my son?"

"Your word bond on the war?"

"Word is bond"

"Your son will be there tomorrow"

"Why not tonight?"

"He's enjoying himself too much"

"Ain't nothing else for us to talk about then, son"

Without a word, KoKo hung up. Enuff said.

In Atlanta, nothing had ever happened like this before, ever. And no one could explain what the hell was the matter.

It was a Friday night and throughout nightclubs and strip joints all across the ATL that were filled with music, the lights low and pulsating with phat-ass bitches, there were no thugs!

Hoes sat alone, in pairs, or in groups at hot spots such as the Atrium, The Velvet Room, Oxygen, Club Vision and everywhere else in Hotlanta that the beautiful people congregated to see and to be seen, but it had never been empty of thugs. Usually thugs were wall to wall in the flyest gear and sporting the freshest haircuts, but not tonight and for the most part it didn't look like they were going to show up at all. Not tonight, anyway.

The owner of Goose Bumps tried to shrug it off. "They'll be here, ladies. Be patient"

At The Pink Pony, drinks were on the house until the thugs arrived while at The Crow's Nest the women played a game they made up called, *Where In The Hell Are The Thugs!*

"Wonderful!," the manager of Body Tap grumbled around midnight before deciding to close down for the night. "Motherfucking wonderful!"

Everyone was furious because without the thugs, the entertainment circuit would lose countless dollars since it was thug money that powered the nightlife, pouring small fortunes into drinks and the other party favors that came along with a night out on the town.

This shit was crazy, damn near a violation of everything a thug motherfucka represented. Niggas know that the weekend was their time to shine and drop paper. That was the law in Thugville.

Shit was crazy.

There were three chartered buses and each bus was filled with Atlanta thugs headed for the Yadkin River Valley in North Carolina. Motherfuckas were rolling with the South! They were going to do the North, finish them niggas once and for all. It was getting ready to go down.

The thugs from Atlanta had stuffed the luggage compartment of the bus with every type of weapon available from handguns to assault rifles, from shotguns to machetes and swords.

Each of the ATL thugs wore sinister looking red and black T-shirts with the work CRUNK written in large letters across the front with the face of Lil' Jon on the back.

The buses rolled through the midnight blackness.

Up I-85.

Ahead of the Atlanta crew and about an hour farther up the Interstate was a caravan of thugs from Rock Hill and other parts of South Carolina. The Greenville posse was rolling in from up I-77, all of them heading for the grape patch in North Carolina.

In Memphis, even though the curfew still had the city on lock, the thugs violated it. They fled the city. Their destination: The Grape Patch.

The reaction in the North was equally bloodthirsty as both Philly and New Jersey relented, sending out large contingents of thugs to aid and assist the North. Only DC chose to remain neutral, committed to the principle of not fighting which is how they viewed North Carolina, but other thug havens stepped up.

Hardly uninterested in the Thug War, Boston, Delaware, and Connecticut sent reinforcements. Even tiny Rhode Island had a thug recruitment drive and sent niggas and guns down to the Grape Patch to help fuck up the South.

Everyone arrived on Saturday.

One day left.

Sunday.

Early.

On Saturday, Justice took to the grape patch early. The morning had dawned crisp and clear, the Carolina sky blue, but Justice was more concerned about the earth than the clouds. To the left and right of him, Justice had his soldiers testing the texture and firmness of the ground so they would know what type of shoe would provide the best traction on the surface. It was a sure bet the grass, in the early morning hours, would be wet and slick with dew and Justice wanted to avoid the embarrassment of his thugs losing their footing when the battle raged hot and hand-to-hand combat was required.

Both sides had been supplied maps and Justice studied his intently. He went over it with Stephon, trying to decide where they should locate their main supply route, finally agreeing on a narrow path running north. There they would set up their medical tents and next to it, their arsenal depot which would be less visible to the Southern thugs if it was surrounded with their supply trucks.

Justice wasn't sure how long the battle would last, but he was sure he could finish off his rival thugs without his supplies being stretched too far. At least, he prayed that was the case.

Stephon, a tested war veteran from the Bronx, wisely pointed to the spot on the map best suited for the North to erect their Commander's station. The small area rose at a very slight angle up a grass incline about a hundred yards from the perimeter of their encampment. Justice liked the vantage point as it would permit him a bird's-eye view of the battlefield which would allow him to command his troops while being able to see exactly what was happening as it took place in real time.

In the meanwhile, Justice had to confront the inevitable question of a retreat and though he did not want to admit to the need for such recourse as the top War Dawg, he was duty bound to have an escape route established. From his studies, Justice understood that a retreat had to be conducted as orderly as any other aspect of the battle because nothing was as unattractive or smacked of cowardice more than an out of control army running while their enemy sold death to them from the rear.

"What about a RETREAT?"

To his credit, Stephon didn't flinch, but neither did he give an instant answer.

"Gotta be dealt with," Justice acknowledged somberly, "and since we can't ignore it we just as well handle it now"

Stephon smirked. "Yeah, why not, but I don't like it. You know why? 'Cause it is a goddamn contradiction, son. In a for real war, you fight to the motherfucking death, to the last man. That's war. A motherfucka know that he gotta put in mad work or else he gonna get slumped"

To his own surprise, Stephon's tone turned venomous, filled with acid and hate. "In the old days when a warrior went out to battle, his woman would greet the motherfucka at the front of the tent and hand him his shield and tell the motherfucka to either come home with his shield or on it-------

213

dead. Unless it could be justified, a warrior who came back from battle without his shield was looked upon without suspicion. People would believe that he had dropped his shield and run like a Bitch"

"What they do to him?" Justice asked.

Stephon shrugged. "Depends on the situation, see what I'm saying? Anyway, man, how you gonna train your soldiers to fight to the motherfucking bitter end when at the same goddamn time, you telling them how to run if the shit get too hot for 'em? That's a contradiction, see what I'm saying, son? You telling your boys to hold the fort down, but you babying the motherfuckas by giving them a backdoor to run through if they see they coming up short"

"I'm feeling that, son" Justice confessed. "No doubt"

"It's like how a nigga gonna fight hard when he got his eye on the goddamn backdoor. Motherfucka can't rumble 'cause his mind halfway on the getaway whereas if his undercover coward ass didn't have that option, he'd stand tall and battle like Chake Zulu" Stephon looked at Justice. "Tell me something, son, how you gonna trust your pit bull to guard your crib the second time when he laid down on the job the first time and let your spot get crashed? Motherfucka sleep or slip one time, he'll do it again. Same thing with a soldier, he retreat one time and he ain't no mo' good. Get running in his blood and motherfucka might give you one round of good fighting and then he ready to take a dive"

Justice reassured Stephon. "Naw, our boys ain't like that. It's them country niggas' hearts that pump Kool-Aid"

Stephon smiled, but he wasn't totally convinced. "I give big Ups to what our niggas from up North have done so far, but the power of suggestion a bitch. You plant the wrong seed and shit will start to fall a-goddamn-part before you know what the fuck don' gone wrong. So far, niggas have put in work without the benefit of a retreat plan, but once you introduce that idea", Stephon shrugged. "See what I'm saying, son? You know what the Muslims used to do? They would dig in and then tie their legs together tightly. This way, they had no choice but to win or die. Couldn't run"

"Don't worry, Stephon, our boys ain't gonna run either"

Stephon saluted but without much enthusiasm. He was a firm believer that time would tell.

At the first sight of the New York niggas, Coot and the Southern masses didn't show any visible concern about their assumed aggressiveness or take-no-prisoner attitude.

"I can't see it," Big Hank snarled, "them niggas getting off on us. Man, we gonna leak them niggas something terrible. The North done finally met they match"

Coot stared at them with great interest. "They are worthy, trust me" When Big Hank attempted to persuade him otherwise, Coot reminded him of what havoc New York had wreaked on the South up to this point. "And that was before they had Jersey, Philly, and them other hoods riding wit' 'em" When Big Hank reacted with utter silence, Coot grinned. "Now that everything is back into prospective, I advise everyone to pay damn close attention to what them niggas do 'cause they setting up they battle plans, so if we stay on top of their movements we might get some info that will help us to decipher they cipher and peep they plan of attack" Coot looked directly at Big Hank as he spoke. "Whatever you do, I beg you not to take them niggas lightly"

Using binoculars, Rip and Moto intently observed the enemy movement, explaining to Coot what was going on across the grape patch. Later, this interpretation of events would be pondered and then hammered into a counteroffensive.

"They know we're checking them out, Moto conceded, so a lot of what they do will be bullshit, meant to trick us into a faulty attack plan. What we get now may not be what we'll see in the morning"

"So when we go out this evening to case the killing floor, we gonna have to be tricky ourselves. They gonna be checking us out bigtime so we gotta fake 'em out of their motherfucking shoes" Rip ran his hand over his head. "We can't let our shit get peeped or else they will be able to counter"

"No matter what they do," Coot declared firmly, "they will lose. The Grape Patch will be their resting place, so help me God"

Chapter 19

Rah-Rah had no intention of departing New York until he had seen his son with his own eyes and had embraced him warmly, welcoming him back home, but now that Rah 3 had been returned safely, the Governor had forbidden Rah-Rah to visit the Grape Patch. Without saying much, Gov. Rand had merely suggested that Rah-Rah remain in Westchester County until further notice. He assured Rah-Rah that he had personally tracked the New York troop formation and informed him like a proud father that Justice had positioned the Northern thugs with a shrewd military genius. All would go well, the Governor had said.

Finding himself stuck in New York, Rah-Rah went to work at setting up the administrative offices necessary to implement order as soon as he gained control of the South. He had to set up an interim government, complete with enforcement power, to maintain and support the security force he would establish to restore immediate peace.

Rah-Rah had it all planned. A new, unified Thug Kingdom was about to rise out of the ashes of the Yadkin River Valley and he was exhilarated, having known no greater joy in his life. He thought about that and conceded that yes this superceded even the wonder of Rah 3's birth and the adventure of getting his first piece of pussy.

In a sudden fit of ecstasy, Rah-Rah fell to his knees, his eyes wet with tears, and lifted up his hands in solemn supplication.

"I will rule wisely, Heavenly Father," he proclaimed loudly. "I vow to protect and defend those who serve me, but will deal harshly with those who defy me. Oh Lord, may the thug Nation prosper and last forever!"

At a little bit before dawn, Coot, dressed in camouflage with one of the Crunk T-shirts, rode out to the front to holla at his troop generals, Rip and Moto, for the last time before the bugle would sound, bringing on the noize of the Thug War.

Coot's heart swelled with pride as he inspected the Southern troops and damn near every hood in the Bottom had sent soldiers. Even Miami and New Orleans represented!

Searching for Bay-Bay. Coot summoned the young thug from Raleigh before him. Coot had promised to let the brace, young fifteen year thug lead his own youth division and Coot kept his promise. Dramatically, Coot yanked the CRUNK T-shirt over his head and carefully affixed it to a long pole until he had transformed the shirt into a red and black banner which, when held aloft, fluttered in the gentle breeze like a menacing flag.

The South let loose a might cheer.

Directly behind Coot were heavily armed thugs from Charlotte, many of whom represented what had been left of

KoKo's own Westside Connection. The others came from North Charlotte, Grier Town, Cherry and Southside. Coot wanted them front and center so they could lead the charge.

To the immediate right of Charlotte was the highly ferocious fighting machine from the ATL. The brothas would be hard to slow down once they got crunked and it was a known fact that they didn't believe in going backwards in battle. All these niggas knew was "full steam ahead"

Left of center were die-hard trooper thugs from South Carolina and Tennessee while the seasoned vets from Florida and Louisiana brought up the rear. Bay-Bay's 'shorty' division would cover the flanks of the entire Southern regiment to prevent the North from executing any sneak attacks through their backdoor.

Having foreseen and seen through all the tactical ploys of the North on yesterday Coot was satisfied with the troop formation of the Southern thugs.

"Send them niggas home dead," he commanded.

Justice despised Southern thugs, thought they were all country and hadn't earned enough respect to be regarded as genuine gangstas. Today, he would smash the niggas. First, he would take out their southern flank, then collapse their center and after he had halted their forward advance he would cripple their rear guard. Then he would destroy them one by one.

Gazing into the sky, Justice could discern that soon the black thread of darkness would give way to the oncoming brightness of day, and soon the moment would be upon him. He motioned to his left column and D-Dot moved a phalanx of shotgun-toting niggas from Queens to the front line. He wanted guns close by that made a lot of noise and that did a lot of damage. Behind them he lined up, the BK hood with their fully automatic assault rifles. He wanted constant fire, an unrelenting blitz and barrage of shell and buckshot that would shock and awe the South.

Looking his troops over, Justice fell into position.

"For them niggas," he said, "the end is near"

It was just before dawn and though he hadn't had time to assess the danger, KoKo felt he had something to fear. Just what. He had no idea yet. In fact, he had no idea why he was in New York City at this time of morning except that Gov. Monroe had ordered him here, telling him nothing more than it was something there that had to be attended to. KoKo had his gun.

Despite his protest of driving down from Connecticut so early in the morning, KoKo's excuses were ignored by Gov. Monroe who promised that a big prize awaited him in New York, so KoKo knew that whatever it was it had something to do with Rah-Rah which also meant he had to be careful. He had no intention of being easy like Sunday morning even though he felt his position was weakened by being on his enemies' turf. And he had heard the rumors of how New York had no love for strangers, but when he thought about it, he did not truly consider himself a stranger. He was more of a conqueror. To be 100% precise, he was more than a conqueror, if you wanted to get biblical.

It was almost dawn when he stepped on the Brooklyn Bridge and Lower Manhattan was being gently tickled by a soft warm breeze that seemed to blow in the opposite direction before bouncing off of City Hall.

Walking slowly, KoKo was so alert that he could instantly feel, without looking, when the concrete platform turned into plank. Traffic grew more and more distant. KoKo kept walking. And walking.

Hardly paying much attention to the skyline, KoKo absorbed himself in deep thought, purposefully trying to recall all of the Governor's instruction while to the south he stole a quick peek at the AIG Building with the needle top. He smelled the water, and kept on walking.

Pausing momentarily to watch the barges and tugs float lazily on the East River, he experienced a sense of time slowing down, so he looked away to only discover that gazing at the giant ferries on Staten Island induces virtually the same identical surrealistic frame of mind where life streamed past in super slo-mo. To counter this dazed perspective, KoKo jogged to the base of the tower on the bridge. He stopped, caught his breath, looked up and saw Governor Monroe emerging from a small group of picture snapping tourists.

"Top of the morning to you, Mr. Combs" The Governor was smiling as he extended his hand. "The early bird catches the worm and what better place to catch a worm than in an apple. A Big Apple"

KoKo was not amused, "What is this all about, Governor?"

"What is it that they say, Mr. Combs, that the darkest hour is just before dawn?"

"I wouldn't know or care about that, Governor," KoKo sighed. "I'm not much of a morning person"

"But I'm willing to bet that may soon change. Today is a day you won't soon forget, but come on, we must hurry back to Manhattan. There's a show coming on at dawn that I don't want you to miss. Come, come, Mr. Combs. We must be quick"

Suddenly KoKo felt like a pawn in whatever game the Governor was playing.

In contrast to KoKo, Rah-Rah who felt like he owned the world, played right along with Governor Rand. It had taken him about five minutes to figure out what this was all about, so he went along willingly because it delighted him to know that at the end of the journey he would come face to face with Charlotte, the motherfucka who had jacked his son. And he was going to swiss cheese that nigga up. For that reason alone, there was a heated up sense of drama in the air that was so pulsating that it throbbed like a drum in his ears.

He touched the butt of his .45.

Walking back past the South Street Seaport, KoKo felt like he had just parachuted behind enemy lines, but also that this was one mission where the enemy was somehow expecting him. KoKo grimaced. This was a personal odyssey, a private adventure with more than enough electricity to power the remainder of his life, that is, if he managed to survive. And he would.

"Where the fuck we going, Governor?"

At first Governor Monroe acted upset with the question. He frowned but not a heartbeat later was sporting a wide-assed grin. "I bet you were the kind of kid who opened your presents on Christmas Eve, couldn't goddamn wait until Santa Claus had gone"

"It's just that I got other thangs to do today"

"Ain't that a bitch because so the hell do I"

KoKo stopped walking. "Is this some sort of trap or---"

"I beg your pardon"

"Is this a goddamn trap," KoKo said loudly, "that's what the fuck I said"

The Governor's face took on a pained expression. "Have I led you into any goddamn traps so far? Personally, I think I've been doing a pretty good job of saving your cookies up to this point"

"Chill out, man. I had to ask. It ain't often I get a call to stroll along the Brooklyn Bridge at dawn"

"It's not dawn yet"

"Soon will be"

"Then we had better hurry so you won't miss your surprise"

Now KoKo was sure Rah-Rah would be waiting.

At Church and Dey Streets in front of the Millennium Hotel, Rah-Rah underwent a mind-numbing emotional experience. This was it. And when that thought came, the thrill was both spiritual and sexual, making his dick hard while at the same time sending a spasm of cold chills up his spine and into his brain. That's how addicted he was to the concept of killing Charlotte.

Adrenaline and anxiety, wrapped together, flooded his chest, pounding against his heart like the Hammer of Thor, but Rah-Rah wasn't interested at the unintended side effects. All he knew is that he could hardly wait to put one in Charlotte's head. He fingered his gun once more. It was ready to bust.

Concluding that this is where it would all end, Rah-Rah took a long, deep breath and smiled. "What are we waiting for?"

Governor Rand opened the door to the hotel's lobby. "Thugs first"

When KoKo stepped into the lobby of the Millennium Hotel he felt his pulse quickening and before he even realized he had changed, he was transformed into a predator. With his sensory perceptions on red alert it took only a half second for KoKo to recognize that no one in the lobby was concerned about him, but he knew he couldn't afford the luxury of standing still to sort shit out because until things made sense it would be wiser to be a moving target, harder to hit.

A brief period of panic seized KoKo when he turned around to find that Governor Monroe had vanished. That left him to find his way to the restaurant on his own. He adjusted his weapon so that it would be easier to reach and he thanked God that Kendra had made him wear his bullet-proof vest because he expected the bullets to start flying any minute now since at this stage of the game anything else would be relatively pointless. He wanted to kill Rah-Rah. Rah-Rah wanted to kill him.

Bullets.

Sweat dripped off the tip of Rah-Rah's nose. He was all alone now, but that didn't change a damn thing because his sole objective as well as the temporary reason for his existence was to D.O.A. (Dead On Arrival) Charlotte. Everything else he discounted. This was bigger than pussy or paper. This was the ultimate mission.

Moving down the hallway, Rah-Rah's life flashed before his eyes like a 3-D movie filled with hoes, clothes, money and cars, proof positive that he was indeed a baller.

224

Rah-Rah mentally applauded himself. His life as a thug has been a magnificent work of art and he was prepared to die if it came to that, but I wouldn't.

Charlotte would die instead.

The hallway was disappointingly short and before he knew it, KoKo felt as if the color scheme had jumped ship on him, going from bright, open hues to more darker earth tones, but all of this was irrelevant. The restaurant, if it existed, was right around the corner to the left. And that was where he needed to be.

KoKo's gun was now in his hand.

On the other end of the hallway, Rah-Rah stepped into the hotel's weight room. There he withdrew the .45 from its holster, ejected the clip and then upon close inspection, slammed it back into place. He also took a second to adjust his bullet-proof vest for a snugger fit. Now, he was primed for war.

Instinctively, he could sense that his prey was near, could almost smell his blood, could visualize his murder. Rah-Rah stood in the gym for a second longer, getting connected to the feel and power of his .45 and now with his kill turned UP on LOUD, he saw no point in keeping his glory waiting. He stepped back out.

The movement was too fast for him and Rah-Rah reacted to it much slower than he would have ever thought he would, but by the time he had gotten his gun up, he found himself in a deadly predicament.

225

What he heard next was a two-word command: "Drop It!"

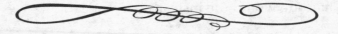

Now that his state was altered, KoKo moved with a fluid grace. He scarcely seemed to feel his feet glide across the carpeted floor. He was so smooth he wanted to laugh.

All the way down the hallway, everything fit into one perfect picture since already he had tapped into the heat of the kill. His mind was a void and his enemy would soon be on the way to hell. Just like it was magic.

KoKo turned left at the corner. He was instantly overwhelmed. Mission Impossible, he thought, as he was disarmed, shoved up against the wall, and frisked thoroughly.

What part of the game was this!

Chapter 20

When KoKo was escorted into the restaurant, Rah-Rah was already there sitting in a chair at the bar facing a gigantic flat-screened TV. Sensing who KoKo was, he attempted to leap up and lunge at his adversary, but he was easily restrained by the other armed men in the closed establishment.

"Sit his ass right here"

KoKo was shoved into a seat next to Rah-Rah's.

"I'd advise both of you to use your fool heads," the mountain of a black man said gruffly, "because if either of you act uncivilized in my presence, I will order you shot in the head" He stepped into the tiny space between Rah-Rah and KoKo and bent his head down, but not bothering to lower his voice. "Both of you are commanded to sit the fuck still, ignore each other, and pay close attention to the television screen. Do you thug motherfuckas understand?"

Both men nodded.

"That pleases me immensely", he snarled. Starting to turn away, he didn't. "Believe it or not, today could end up becoming the luckiest day of your thuggish-assed lives"

"It's dawn, sir"

The man nodded. "Hit the switch" The man moved away as the silver-framed TV exploded on with a burst of vivid, spectacular, unimaginable color. "What we have, gentlemen, is satellite. I think you may recognize those illustrious stars in this epic saga"

Both KoKo and Rah-Rah gasped in stunned, utter amazement. It was The Grape Patch! And there on the huge screen were the North and the South thugs in battle formation. Neither man had ever seen anything quite like this, could hardly believe their eyes, but when Rah-Rah, through cracked, dry lips begged for sound, the battle and hum of the Grape Patch thundered ON. The battle was loud and maddening, aptly befitting what was about to occur. M & M. Mayhem and Murder.

KoKo's voice caught in his throat as he observed Coot readying the Southern Thugs. They looked well-prepared and disciplined, eager to give death to the up North niggas up and stretched out across the vineyard from them. KoKo could read the triumph on their faces as they awaited the bugle to sound, opening the assault.

Yet to consider defeat, Rah-Rah saw that Justice had chosen his captains wisely and it only added to his glee when he saw that Philly and Jersey had sent out their bravest warriors to aid and assist in this glorious Thug War. They would be rewarded handsomely. No doubt.

Rah-Rah was also glad to see that Justice had included more sawed-off, pump shotguns to their arsenal. These pieces were essentially cannons.

The color was so clear that KoKo could practically feel the temperature and intimately experience the weather in the

Yadkin River Valley. That's how alive the screen was. KoKo also sensed that this was a battle he would win.

All of a sudden, the screen went totally silent as thugs on both sides withdrew within themselves, going numbly into the zone, that space where their warrior resided.

The tension in the room was as equally great as everyone knew that only a few seconds were left before the clash. KoKo and Rah-Rah watch in rapt attention as both sides glared through vacant eyes across the Grape which shortly would be slippery with blood and the mangled bodies of the dead.

Coot raised his hand high in the air. Then in a swift violent motion, yanked it down.

The bugle sounded.

CHARGE!!!

Both sides, North and South, bum rushed each other, moving quicker, faster, than either had expected or anticipated. At first, it appeared that the thugs on both sides were acting on impulse, blinded by bloodlust, but within a matter of seconds the strategy became clear as the thugs took up their assigned position in the staging area of the battlefield.

The roar of gunfire thundered, but from this frantic beginning it was difficult to see who was getting the better of it. Bodies fell like rain. South and North.

Rah-Rah and KoKo were both now standing, staring opened mouth as the thugs fanned out, desperately hoping for a breach in their enemies' formation, but both sides held firm, giving nothing.

Then Rah-Rah gasped as the first explosion went off, digging up the ground under his men feet, swallowing them up like a tom cat gulps a goldfish, but before KoKo could cheer the new development, he noticed the strange, puzzled look on Coot's face. Looking at the ground, KoKo understood that Coot felt the earth moving under his feet. Then the next horrible explosion came. KoKo choked when he witnessed Coot's body shredded into a thousand fragments by the landmine.

After a few seconds respite, the explosions resumed, killing thugs on both sides.

"Oh my God!", Rah-Rah screamed, "What's happening?!"

Turn it off", the big, black man ordered and instantly the screen faded to empty. No sound. He confronted KoKo and Rah-Rah. "You both lost. End of story. Not a single thug will get out of there alive. Those who do somehow escape the landmines that were secretly planted will be mowed down like dogs. By whom is none of your business"

"Why?" Rah-Rah croaked.

"I find that question facetious. Why, you ask? Why the fuck not, but even that doesn't take much thought. Weren't you two planning on wiping each other out. Don't hate us because we did it for you. Oh, I get it. There was supposed to be a winner, wasn't there?" The big man shrugged. "What good is bragging rights if you're too dead to brag?"

"I don't believe this shit", KoKo groaned.

"Believe it, young brotha"

"You set us up", Rah-Rah ranted.

`The big man laughed. "You call it setting you up. I call it shutting you niggas down, but by whatever name it's called, it was effective and not only that, it has brought the thug world to and end. That's it, guys. The entire Thug Nation just got erased. We dismissed y'all silly niggas like you were a bunch of bitches, but there's good news"

"What?", KoKo asked.

"You two are still alive so unlike all of your associates. That should count for something"

"I hope you're not expecting me to kiss your ass", Rah-Rah cracked, "cause it ain't happening"

"Getting my ass kissed doesn't turn me on, youngblood, but we do have plans for both of you. And neither of you will be compelled in any way to join us. As a matter of fact, both of you will be free to go your merry way to do as you very well please. If you like, you can recruit another bunch of niggas to thug with you. That's on you, but we're giving you an opportunity to do something affirmative with the rest of your lives"

"Such as?"

"First", Rah-Rah interjected, "Who are you motherfuckas?"

"Good questions"

"Well, answer it then"

"Simply put, we're a secret organization of brothas who have negotiated a deal with Uncle Sam"

"Like the government is gonna keep its word to a bunch of niggas" KoKo glared at the man. "Evidently, you don't know your black history"

"I carefully considered the government's previous duplicity in their dealings with us before I made this deal. It's ironclad and it will be honored"

Rah-Rah laughed. "Bullshit"

"You let us lose sleep over that. What you two need to do is to decide if you want to take advantage of the golden opportunity being offered to you. You both saw it, The Thug World is officially destroyed and to be honest we'll never allow it to rise again"

"There will always be thugs, "Rah-Rah bragged, just like there'll always be lawyers and doctors. Can't stop that, thugs are as much a part of America as congressmen"

231

"You might have a point there, but right now all that's out there right now are has-beens and wannabees. Real thugs, you two, are the last ones left" The big man grinned, his eyes bright. "We had to sacrifice the thugs for the overall good of our survival as a people and believe me, thuggish behavior will never again be tolerated. This is a new day for the black man in America, this is the beginning of our own New World Order"

KoKo smirked mirthlessly. "Crackers ain't gonna let niggas build nuthin' in this country"

Rah-Rah nodded. "I agree with that. America is the white man's cipher. Niggas can't build here"

The big man looked impatient. "Look, I know this has been an ordeal for you and right now, the reality of what has happened hasn't truly set in yet, but it was real. That was no video game or movie you saw. All of your friends are dead. Thugs are no more", he sighed. "We spared you two because both of you are true leaders and we can use you in the development of our historic plan to resurrect the black man in America. Yes, we need you"

KoKo shook his head. "You set us up"

"It was done to save the rest of us, so we look at it as a racial necessity, something that had to be done because it was better that a few of us die than all of us"

"And you saw us as some kind of threat to your so-called New World Order?", Rah-Rah scowled. "Is that it?"

"Actually we didn't give a damn about you being a threat to the white folks because they had jails and prisons, but once you got to be too big a problem is when they came to us, offering all kinds of inducements to contain the thug menace. Shit, we didn't know what to do, but you guys personally gave us the shot we needed when you decided to go to war with one another. It was the perfect scenario. We simply took advantage of a situation you guys"

"What now? You sound mighty proud of what you've done, but what comes next?"

The big man appeared jacked up, amped emotionally. "The white man has been most generous. He has given us the reparations money"

"We-we got it?", KoKo asked. "Reparations?"

"Hold on, youngblood, when I say we, I mean we" The big man made gesture that both Rah-Rah and KoKo understood to mean that the 'we' the man spoke of was the organization he ran.

"So that's how it goes?", Rah-Rah exclaimed. "That's some Judas shit"

"I wasn't sure whether I should have told you that or not because I knew you'd get it fucked up, but here's the deal. We, my organization, will get the money and we'll use it to develop the African-American community. The rest of the brothas and sistas won't even know about the money. This way the confusion can be kept down. Plus if niggas got the money, the white man would get it right back anyway"

"So you're the president of Nigga America?"

"No, I'm simply an administrator for the disbursement of the funds. We will build our own schools, our own hospitals, our own businesses"

"It's a goddamn dream", Rah-Rah shouted, "because niggas won't spend with niggas"

"Really? Then that's where you two come in. Both of you are leaders and we need people like you to open the eyes and to prepare the minds of the masses. We need to join with Russell Simmons because we need to Rock the Vote to put our own candidates into office. We also must focus on overturning mandatory minimums in this country so brothas and sistas can get out of prison. We need to join up with those sistas down at Spelman College to help reclaim and restore the image of the black woman" The big man paused. "If either of you have ever heard of Dr. Claud Anderson or his book Powernomics, then this is his program in action"

Rah-Rah grunted.

"We have 10 years, my brothas, to get our shit together. Ten years"

"Then what?"

"Then the rest of us die"

"Like that?" KoKo pointed at the TV screen.

"Or something like that" The big man swallowed. "However it comes, it won't be pretty. Thugs today. The rest of us in a decade if we fail to float our own boat. Please don't think this is a gimmick that I have cooked up. It's real. The white man is tired of us and we have become a burden he is willing to unload. They are finished paying our way, so we take this chance and make it or we die" The big man shrugged. "You have 72 hours to think it over.

Standing outside Rah-Rah didn't seem to give a damn one way or the other.

"I'm in," KoKo said. "And you?"

"Fuck that nigga. I'm a thug for life. That bullshit he was talking didn't impress me at all. Plus, I don't need nobody giving me no special privileges no how. I know how to get what I want"

"Crackers might not be gaming"

"Go 'head on back South, nigga. You done gave up your thughood, so I see you as a traitor. All your boys gone and you ready to start wearing a suit and a tie. That's bitch shit"

"So you don't believe this the end of the thug world as we know it"

"Hell naw, nigga, because as long as there is one thug in the world, there's a thug world and being that the one thug is me, I'm still representing. Long live a true thug and may all the dead ones rest in peace"

"So, it's possible that we may meet again in battle?"

"You better hope not, nigga"

"Yeah, one of us better hope not"

Rah-Rah squared up. "We ain't gotta wait, son. We can do this right here, right now"

"Man, you crazy and to be honest I hope I don't never see you ever again in life"

"That'll probably be best"

"Rah-Rah, nigga. I'm out. Peace"

Rah-Rah teased. "You gonna get drunk?"

"Naw, nigga, I'm gonna get CRUNK!", KoKo stuck out his fist for some dap, "The second episode is coming"

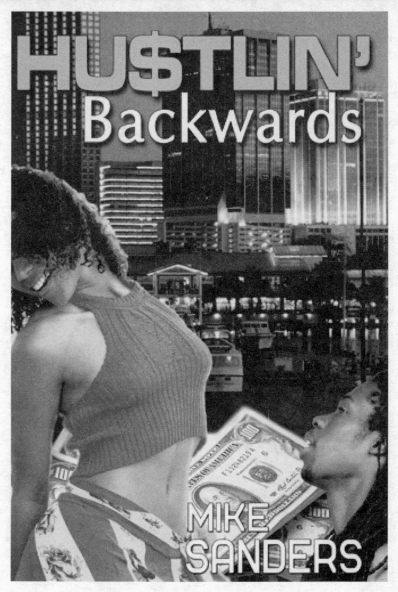

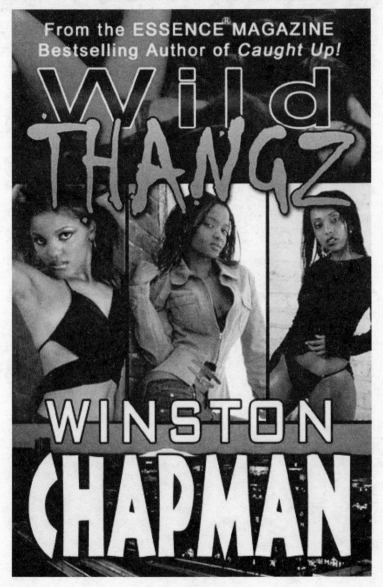

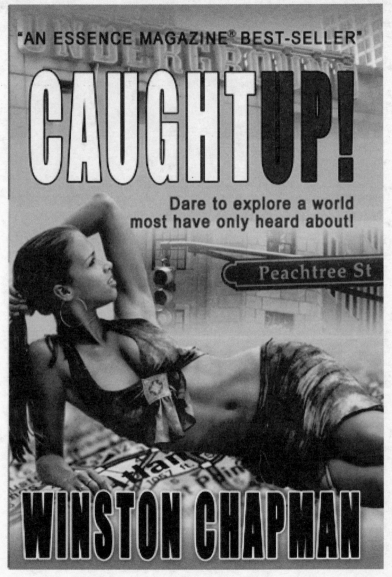

BLACK PEARL BOOKS INC.

ORDER FORM

Black Pearl Books Inc.
3653-F Flakes Mill Road - PMB 306
Atlanta, Georgia 30034
w w w . B l a c k P e a r l B o o k s . c o m

YES, We Ship Directly To Prisons & Correctional Facilities
INSTITUTIONAL CHECKS & MONEY ORDERS ONLY!

TITLE	Total
"Caught Up!" by Winston Chapman Quantity: ___ x $ 14.95	
"Sex A Baller" by Mysterious Luva Quantity: ___ x $ 12.95	
"Wild Thangz" by Winston Chapman Quantity: ___ x $ 14.95	
"Crunk" by Bad Boyz Quantity: ___ x $ 14.95	
"Hustlin Backwards" by Mike Sanders Quantity: ___ x $ 14.95	
Sub-Total	$
SHIPPING: ___ # books x $ 3.50 ea. (Via US Priority Mail)	$
GRAND TOTAL	$

SHIP TO:

Name: _____

Address: _____

Apt or Box #: _____

City: _____ State: _____ Zip: _____

Phone: _____ E-mail: _____